PUFFIN BOOKS

THE CHRISTMASAURUS
AND THE
NAUGHTY LIST

THE CHRISTMASAURUS
AND THE
NAUGHTY LiST

TOM FLETCHER

Illustrations by Shane Devries

PUFFIN

PUFFIN BOOKS

UK | USA | Canada | Ireland | Australia
India | New Zealand | South Africa

Puffin Books is part of the Penguin Random House group of companies
whose addresses can be found at global.penguinrandomhouse.com.

www.penguin.co.uk   www.puffin.co.uk   www.ladybird.co.uk

First published 2021
003

Cover, illustrations and text copyright © Tom Fletcher, 2021
Illustrations by Shane Devries

The moral right of the author has been asserted

Set in Baskerville MT Pro
Text design by Mandy Norman
Printed in Great Britain by Clays Ltd, Elcograf S.p.A.

The authorized representative in the EEA is Penguin Random House Ireland,
Morrison Chambers, 32 Nassau Street, Dublin D02 YH68

A CIP catalogue record for this book is available from the British Library

HARDBACK
ISBN: 978–0–241–40735–6

INTERNATIONAL PAPERBACK
ISBN: 978–0–241–40756–1

All correspondence to:
Puffin Books, Penguin Random House Children's
One Embassy Gardens, 8 Viaduct Gardens, London SW11 7BW

For Buzz, Buddy and Max

THE NAUGHTY LIST

Ronnie Nutbog,
who's always been a bully.

**Truly and Utterly
Snottersworth –**
two truly spoilt and utterly
horrid princesses in a
land far, far away.

Marvin Johnson,
otherwise known as
GAMERKIDD3000 –
who *used* to be the best big
brother in the world.

Ella Noying, who never eats a single vegetable (and can't even bear to hear the words 'Brussels sprouts').

Gemolina Shine, who's determined to be a star, no matter what.

AND A SURPRISE ENTRY ON THE NAUGHTY LIST:

William Trundle – the boy who saved Christmas . . . twice!

CONTENTS

1. *Previously on the Christmasaurus*   1

2. *Back to the North Pole*   7

3. *The Shadows of the Naughty List*   16

4. *Breaking Rules*   29

5. *Ronnie Nutbog*   41

6. *Nutbog's Savings*   47

7. *Old Granny Nutbog*   56

8. *Being Nice*   66

9. *Sold!*   75

10. *Truly and Utterly Snottersworth*   84

11. *A Secret Gargoyle*   95

12. *The Royal Toymaker*   106

13. *Royal Passengers*   116

14. *Putting Things Right*   133

15. *Delivering in the Dark*   140

16. *GamerKidd3000*   152

17. *Where It All Went Pong*   161

18. *Feeling So Low, Flying Solo*   171

19. *Christmasaurus3000*   178

20. *Football-o-saurus*   186

21. *Ping Gets His Pong Back*   193

22. *Ella Noying*   213

23. *Dumping Dinner*   223

24. *Sprouts*   232

25. *Ella and the Elves*   243

26. *The Snow Ranch*   256

27. *Buttercream*   265

28. *Gemolina Shine*   280

29. *Whatever It Takes*   290

30. *A Singing Tornado*   304

31. *Encore*   308

32. *Dorothy Dorkins*   316

33. *Showtime*   325

34. *Where's William?*   336

35. *William Trundle*   341

36. *It Gets Worse for William*   352

37. *William and the Christmasaurus*   364

38. *A Blue Hope*   376

39. *Another Tooth*   383

40. *Switcheroo*   390

41. *The Gift of Second Chances*   402

ACKNOWLEDGEMENTS   417

CHAPTER ONE

PREVIOUSLY ON THE CHRISTMASAURUS

Everyone knows about the Naughty and Nice Lists, right? Well, just in case you've had your head buried in a box of tinsel for your whole entire life, let's imagine for a moment that you've been a good kid all year – I know that might be hard for some of you, but just go with me for a minute – and on Christmas Day you wake up to the presents you've wished hardest for since writing your letter to Santa: toy cars, dolls, train sets, video games . . .

BAM!

There they are, wrapped up in loads of glittery paper and ribbons that your parents will spend the rest of Christmas tidying up.

Congratulations – you made it on to the

NICE LIST!

But now imagine what might happen if maybe, just maybe, you did some things that someone could possibly think were *not nice*. Perhaps, even, dare I say it . . . *naughty*?

Well, in that situation, you would wake up on Christmas Day to a very different, very unpleasant sight. There are rumours of children receiving coal instead of toys, or even of piles of reindeer droppings in stockings (don't eat chocolate raisins on Christmas Day . . . trust me)! But the truth is worse. Much worse. *What could be worse than deer poop in a sock?* I hear you ask. So, imagine waking up to find . . .

NO PRESENTS.

Previously on the Christmasaurus

Uh-oh, looks like you're on the

NAUGHTY LIST!

Don't worry – I'm not judging you! After all, it's not up to me who makes it on to the Naughty or Nice List, I'm just an author writing words on this page – I don't have that kind of power! But there is someone who, if the legends are true, sees you when you're sleeping *and* knows when you're awake, and I'd guess if he can do both those things, then he most certainly knows if you've been BAD OR GOOD! I am, of course, talking about the big man himself, father to the season of seasons, Mr Kris Kringle, St Nick, Sinterklaas or, as we shall call him in this book – **SANTA**.

You might think that the Naughty and Nice List is just the difference between getting a pile of toys or a stocking full of fresh air, but it's MUCH MORE important than that. In fact, the very future of Christmas itself depends on children understanding right from wrong, good from bad, naughty from nice. You see, if there weren't children on a Nice List to deliver presents to, Santa wouldn't have a job! He wouldn't have meaning, or a purpose for us all to believe in. And if we don't believe in him, then, well, he wouldn't exist at all. And think of what a disaster that would mean for Christmas!

And I'm not just talking about the presents. Don't get me wrong – Santa loves a good gift more than anyone – but it's not really about the toy.

It's about the JOY.

That warm feeling you get inside as you open up the thing you've most wished for all year. It's pure happiness, and it all came from being nice. THAT'S why Santa brings presents.

Now, if you've read the first two Christmasaurus books: firstly, well done, you're definitely on the Nice List; and, secondly, the following information will come as no surprise. Santa is an enormous, jolly, fantastic person with eyes as deep blue as the Arctic Ocean and a beard as white as ice. He lives in the North Pole in a snow ranch made of pine and in the company of some rather merry, constantly singing elves. And once a year, when he makes his Christmas deliveries, he flies a sleigh pulled by eight Magnificently Magical Flying Reindeer and . . . hmmmm, I'm sure I'm forgetting something important? ONLY JOKING! Of course, that sleigh is led by the creature whose name is sprawled across the front of this book in nice shiny letters: the one and only

CHRISTMASAURUS!

THE CHRISTMASAURUS AND THE NAUGHTY LIST

An icy-blue dinosaur whose egg was discovered frozen solid, deep in the ice mines by Santa's elves many Christmases ago.

The Christmasaurus couldn't always fly, but, thanks to the belief of his best friend, William Trundle, now the special dino can speed through the sky fast enough to make even the most magical reindeer look like Bambi on a frozen lake. So now each year, as Santa delivers presents to all the children who are lucky enough to make it on to the Nice List, it's the Christmasaurus leading the way.

Which brings us back quite nicely to where we started: the Naughty and Nice Lists! Which is what this book is all about. So, now that you've had a little recap, let's begin!

CHAPTER TWO

BACK TO THE NORTH POLE

his story starts in the most Christmassy place in the world – the North Pole. It was the first of December and, under a blanket of swirling greens, blues and purples of the Northern Lights, Santa's Snow Ranch stood like it was posing for a Christmas card. Deep within this cosy pine building, Santa was sitting in his letter-reading room at the foot of an old, crooked Christmas tree – the oldest Christmas tree in the world, in fact – dunking a generously buttered crumpet into a mug of warm custard. *By the way, if you've never tried a crumpet dunked in custard, then you really must – you'll thank me for it!*

WHAM!

A great crash at the window startled Santa, causing him to drop a dollop of yellow custard on to his white beard.

'Blinking baubles!' he grumbled, turning to see what had made such a clatter. 'Oh, Christmasaurus, it's you. I might have known,' Santa said as he stood and threw open the large, stained-glass window to let his dinosaur companion inside.

'If I've told you once, I've told you a hundred times: just because you *can* fly, it doesn't mean you *have* to fly everywhere. We do have doors in the North Pole too!' Santa chuckled and gave the Christmasaurus a little pat on the head as the creature flew through the open window and into the warm room.

The brilliant blue dinosaur landed with a thud, his translucent claws clopping on the wooden floor. He shook off his icy scales like a dog that had just been for a dip in a pond, sending a shower of snowflakes across the room.

'Mind the list!

MIND THE LIST!'

Santa cried, shielding an awfully important-looking book on his desk from being covered in snow.

At the mention of lists, the Christmasaurus bounded across the room to get a glimpse at the names of those who were on the Nice List this year.

'Nothing to get excited about, I'm afraid, Chrissy,' Santa said, settling himself back down at his desk. 'I'm afraid I'm checking the *other* list tonight.'

Santa pointed his buttery finger at the top of the page where the words **THE NAUGHTY LIST** were written in beautiful golden letters. The Christmasaurus's icy mane drooped with sadness.

9

'I know, I know,' Santa said with a sigh. 'I don't like it either, but I'm afraid it has to be checked once now and then a second time on Christmas Eve. Don't ask me why I do it twice, but it says so in that song, so I feel like I should.'

The Christmasaurus slumped even further. He hated knowing that every name on that list was going to get absolutely zilch for Christmas! And, worse still, he hated seeing how sad it made Santa to read through all the naughty names.

'First things first, it's time for the weigh-in!' Santa said nervously, as he lifted his big, beautiful, brass weighing scales on to the desk. The scales were the old-fashioned kind with two bowls dangling on either side: one of them had the word **NICE** engraved into its polished surface, while the opposite bowl was inscribed with the word **NAUGHTY**.

'The weigh-in is the first stage of checking the lists,' Santa said to the Christmasaurus as he adjusted the scales to make them level. 'It's also an indication of just how naughty or nice children have been this year. Hand me the Nice List, please. It's there on the shelf. Chop, chop!'

The Christmasaurus flew over to the bookshelf, scooped up the thick book with **THE NICE LIST** embossed on its spine and dropped it into Santa's open palms. Santa carefully placed it on the Nice side of the weighing scales and the bowl sank under its weight, almost touching the desk. Then Santa turned back to the intimidatingly chunky Naughty List on his desk and cracked his knuckles before heaving the hefty book towards the opposite side of the scales.

'Now, not to worry if the balance is a little off. It's never perfect at the first weigh-in, but by the time we get to Christmas these scales should be even –'

The scales shifted instantly as the Naughty List hit the desk and sent the much lighter Nice List rocketing up towards the ceiling.

'Ho, ho, oh dear . . .'

Santa sighed, gazing at the Nice List, which was rocking precariously on the weighing scale above the Christmasaurus's head. 'This is all wrong. All wrong! I've never seen such an unbalanced first weigh-in. There must be far too many names on the Naughty List!'

The Christmasaurus stared at the heavy book with concern.

'I mean, of course it's impossible for EVERY child to be on the Nice List, but it shouldn't be *this* uneven, even on the first weigh-in! It's about finding that perfect balance, and these scales should be in harmony,' Santa explained, pointing to the totally unbalanced scales on his desk. 'If they stay tipped too far on the Naughty side, there will be no coming back! It's like rolling a snowball down a hill: the bigger it gets, the harder it is to stop, until eventually there might even be . . .' He gulped.

'No Nice List at all!'

The Christmasaurus curled his tail beneath his legs; his icy mane fell flat, and all the magic in the room seemed to vanish for a moment.

'No Nice List means no nice children who need presents delivered, and that means . . . well, a world without me!'

The Christmasaurus turned a pale shade of his usual vibrant blue. A world *without* Santa? Could the future of Christmas actually be at risk?

'I suppose we should take a look and see what some of these children have been up to. Although with this many names, it may take all night . . . Come on – let's read through the Naughty List together,' Santa said.

He noticed that the Christmasaurus was looking a little concerned (to say the least), so, knowing that snacks always cheered up his friend, Santa reached out and snapped a fresh icicle from the top of the window frame and threw it to the Christmasaurus to munch on.

But the moment the Christmasaurus caught the icicle in his mouth, he felt a sharp, zapping sensation searing through one of his bottom front teeth, causing him to drop the snack and roar in pain.

'Goodness me, whatever is the matter?' Santa asked.

The Christmasaurus wasn't sure. He opened his mouth and scooped up the icicle again for another go but as his tooth crunched down . . . **ZAP!**

The pain shot through his mouth again and he leapt back like he'd been given an electric shock.

'Hmmm, I'd better take a look. Open wide,' Santa said, sliding on the pair of thick *oggle-goggles* he wore to make special tiny toys. His eyeballs looked like enormous blue planets as he gazed into the Christmasaurus's gaping mouth. 'Ah, I see the problem. You seem to have

something stuck in your teeth. In fact, you have rather *a lot* of things stuck in your teeth! I think you need a –'

The Christmasaurus quickly snapped his mouth shut. He knew what was coming next and did not want to hear it!

'You need a dent–' Santa was cut off again by the Christmasaurus burying his scaly, scared head in his claws, which is difficult when you're a distant relative of a T-rex.

'Oh, stop being such a Scared-o-saurus,' Santa teased. 'You have to see the DENTIST!'

THE SHADOWS

CHAPTER THREE

THE SHADOWS OF THE NAUGHTY LIST

'**G**umdrop!' Santa boomed, and clapped his hands together.

Before you could say *jingle bells*, a small elf dressed in blue scrubs with the letters **NES** embroidered on the pocket – National Elf Service – appeared in the reading room.

'So sorry that I took so long.
I heard your call – whatever's wrong?'

Gumdrop chimed elfishly.

16

'It appears that our dinosaur friend here has tooth-ache, and I thought it was best to seek advice from an elf professional. After all, I'm Santa, not the Tooth Fairy!' Santa chortled and slapped his thigh.

> **'Absolutely right you are.**
> **I'll sort this out, Santa.**
> **Now, Christmasaurus,**
> **Please say, AHHHH!'**

Gumdrop sang (remember, all elves LOVE to sing whenever they can and especially when it comes to getting jobs done). Then she peered closer as the Christmasaurus reluctantly revealed a row of sharp teeth in a mouth big enough to swallow an elf whole, which of course he would NEVER do!

> **'Well, roast my spuds, what have we here?**
> **So much, so much for me to clear!'**

Gumdrop tutted as she rolled up the sleeves of her scrubs and leant into the Christmasaurus's mouth!

Santa watched in total astonishment as the tiny dentist pulled out a whole feast of festive food that was wedged between the dinosaur's teeth. Gumdrop listed them all with a merry melody as she worked . . .

> 'On the first day of Christmas,
> Stuck in this dino's teeth:
> Twelve candy canes,
> Eleven mince pies,
> Ten pigs in blankets,
> Nine roasted chestnuts,
> Eight gingerbread houses,
> Seven Christmas puddings,
> Six roast potatoes,
> **FIVE BRUSSELS SPROUTS!**
> Four yule logs,
> Three fruit cakes,
> Two stuffing balls . . .'

Unable to help himself, Santa leapt to his feet and at the top of his voice boomed: '*And a partridge in a pear tree!*'

Silence.

If there's one thing a North Pole elf dislikes more than anything else, it's having the final line of their song stolen.

'Sorry. I couldn't resist . . .' Santa said, looking a bit sheepish. 'Well? How's the tooth?'

'THERE'S NO PEAR TREE OR A PARTRIDGE.
Just a lot of undigested garbage!
You haven't brushed, you silly thing.
Your tooth will not be staying in.'

Gumdrop huffed and gave the troublesome tooth a little kick, causing it to wobble and the Christmasaurus to yelp. Gumdrop climbed down her ladder, shaking her head, while the dinosaur rubbed his cheek. There really is nothing worse than toothache, but for a dinosaur who has never brushed his teeth and lives on a diet of candy canes and Christmas treats, it was a miracle he had any teeth left at all.

'Not to worry, my dear dinosaur. Teeth come and go. Give it a little wobble – go on . . . Let's see it!' Santa said excitedly. Why grown-ups love it when you wiggle a wobbly tooth is one of life's great mysteries.

But the Christmasaurus did NOT want to wobble his tooth. He squeezed his mouth shut and shook his head.

'It's his first wobbly tooth.' Santa beamed at Gumdrop like a proud parent, as though Gumdrop, a professional National Elf Service dentist, didn't already know!

The Christmasaurus, however, was not in the least bit excited about losing his first tooth. In fact, the thought of it falling out made his *whole head* feel more wobbly than the tooth was.

> 'Lay off the candy canes a while
> Or there'll be a gap in your dino smile,'

Gumdrop sang, reaching into her pocket and pulling out a stick of celery.

> 'Lots of vegetables in your diet
> Makes a dentist's day nice and quiet.'

She popped the green stick at the Christmasaurus's feet before slipping away, leaving Santa and the

Christmasaurus to get back to their important business.

There wasn't much that the Christmasaurus wouldn't eat, but he would rather eat a sprout from last year's Christmas dinner than a stick of celery!

Seeing the Christmasaurus's nostrils flare with disgust, Santa opened a drawer in his desk to reveal a red telephone. It looked like the kind of phone that was only used in emergencies in cartoons, and it had just one button on it . . . a direct line to the kitchen!

'Hello? Yes, this is a *veg-mergency*,' Santa said into the mouthpiece and chuckled to himself. 'I said *VEG-*mergency! It's a vegetable emer– Oh, never mind. Just hurry!'

Less than three and a half seconds later, there was a knock at the door, and an elf entered the room wearing a frilly apron and pushing what looked like a tiny kitchen on a trolley!

'Ah, Buttercream, what took you so long? We have a stick of celery that needs your immediate attention,' Santa said to his most trusted elf-chef. 'The Christmasaurus is on strict orders to eat more vegetables, but he doesn't seem very keen.'

'Let me see. Hmmm, celery . . .' Buttercream pondered, adjusting her star-shaped spectacles and examining the stick of celery that was almost as tall as she was.

'Do you think you might be able to make it taste a little more fun?' Santa added, winking at the Christmasaurus.

> **'There is nothing less fun**
> **Than a plain stick of celery.**
> **If I'm to transform it,**
> **It must be done cleverly!'**

Buttercream sang, then from the bottom of her trolley she slid out a large recipe book.

'**Ho, ho, ho**, Christmasaurus – you're in for a treat! Buttercream has been known to make swede more scrumptious than sweets; peas more palatable than pecan pie; and kale . . . well, kale is always a bit gross, I suppose – but, still, if anyone can do it, Buttercream can!' Santa said, rubbing his hands together as Buttercream began chopping this, stirring that, dicing over here, slicing over there. It was like watching an artist paint a masterpiece.

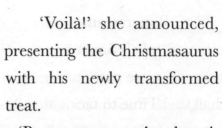

'Voilà!' she announced, presenting the Christmasaurus with his newly transformed treat.

'Buttercream, you've done it again!' Santa beamed, admiring the snack, which now looked like a bejewelled royal sceptre.

'Peanut-butter-stuffed celery
Bejewelled with freshly chopped cherry,
Smooth and yet crunchy, delightfully munchy.
Is it tasty? The answer is: VERY!'

Buttercream smiled as she replaced her recipe book on her trolley and strode out of the door.

'Try it,' Santa said excitedly, and the Christmasaurus took a teeny nibble. Suddenly his tastebuds felt like they were exploding. The celery was sweet, syrupy, salty and savoury all at the same time! He munched up the whole stick of celery and desperately wished there was more.

THE SHADOWS OF THE NAUGHTY LIST

'See, Buttercream makes eating your five-a-day a piece of cake!' Santa winked. 'Hopefully now we can stop any more nasty toothaches! So, let's get back to it, shall we? Time to tackle that Naughty List! Would you be a good dinosaur and dim the lights?'

While Santa heaved the Naughty List from the scales back to the middle of his desk, the Christmasaurus flew around the room in a flash, creating a gust of wind in his wake that blew out the warm glow from the lanterns. Darkness engulfed the room.

Then, once the Christmasaurus had landed, Santa clicked his forefinger and thumb together. He caught a spark of stardust that fell from his hand and lit a dark green candle that was sitting in the centre of his desk.

At the first flash of a flame, the thick woven cover of the Naughty List swung open as though under the command of a magic spell, revealing name after name on page after page, in inky letters that appeared as if being scrawled by the hand of a ghost.

'Let's begin with ... Ronnie Nutbog.' Santa had barely whispered the boy's name before the green candle's flame flickered as though it were dancing in a breeze.

The candlelight started to form shapes and movements on the ceiling that clearly resembled a person – the shadows of the Naughty List.

'Oh yes, I remember Ronnie. He's been quite a regular face on the Naughty List, I'm afraid.' Santa sighed. He and the Christmasaurus watched the dancing shadow of Ronnie Nutbog hold out his hand while other smaller shadow-figures appeared and reluctantly handed over something golden and glowing.

'Stealing lunch money,' Santa whispered. 'No wonder he's on the list again this year.'

The shadows danced on the ceiling, and the scene changed to show Ronnie stashing his stolen cash in some kind of box.

'Next!' Santa boomed. His voice disrupted the flame, causing the candlelight to flicker and make room for the next Naughty-Listers.

Parker Jax Falcone.

Cooper Jones.

Summer Rae Cawley.

The Shadows of the Naughty List

Kit Judd.

Buddy Fletcher.

Orli Daren.

Santa sent up name after name into the air, and shadow after shadow appeared on the ceiling, revealing children at their naughtiest – a girl sneaking out of her house at night; a boy running through his school with no clothes on; twins who wouldn't stop fighting . . . The list went on and on. Checking it was a long, difficult task, but it was about to get a whole lot worse. Even Santa, the man who had seen everything, wasn't ready for the name that was about to appear on the Naughty List.

The golden, ghostly scribed letters reflected in Santa's blue eyes as he began reading them, then his white beard twitched as the Naughty List revealed the child's last name, and Santa's whispered words became a stunned gasp strong enough to suck out the flame of the green candle.

The room plunged into darkness, but not before both Santa and the Christmasaurus had seen the unmistakable shadow of someone they both knew very well flicker across the ceiling in his wheelchair . . .

William Trundle
was on
THE
NAUGHTY
LIST!

CHAPTER FOUR

BREAKING RULES

HOLD IT! Let's rewind for a nanosecond – William Trundle, as some of you may remember, is the nicest, kindest, bravest kid on the planet. He and the Christmasaurus are like peanut butter and celery: at first glance they are total opposites, but together they make the ultimate team and, due to their Christmas adventures, William is almost as famous as Santa in the North Pole –

the boy who saved Christmas . . .

TWICE!

Surely *the* William Trundle wouldn't do something naughty, would he?!

'It can't be true,' Santa whispered nervously in the dark. 'It's . . . it's . . . not possible. Little Willypoos would never, ever, ever do anything bad enough to get himself on the Naughty List.'

The Christmasaurus paced back and forth frantically in the darkness, his claws scratching at the ancient pine floor. Santa was right: William was the Christmasaurus's best friend and would never, ever, ever do anything bad enough to get himself on the Naughty List. Something must have gone horribly wrong. Perhaps William was in trouble!

While the dinosaur worried, Santa clicked his fingers a few times, snapping out a spark of fresh stardust to relight the candle.

As the flame ignited and the shadow of William reappeared, the Christmasaurus angled his mane of pale blue icicles so they caught the candlelight like prisms, sending shards of rainbow beams into the room and extinguishing William's shadow.

'I'm afraid it will take more than a ray of light to take

someone off the Naughty List,' Santa said with a voice full of sorrow.

The Christmasaurus huffed determinedly and growled in the direction of the book.

'I can't! I'm not allowed to interfere!'

Santa said, able to understand the Christmasaurus as easily as reading the candlelight shadows. 'I don't want to see our dear friend on the Naughty List any more than you do. In fact, I'd give the whole Naughty List presents if I could, but there are rules, and if children misbehave they *put themselves* on the list. I can't just hop down chimneys dashing out presents willy-nilly. I'm not the Easter Bunny! I've sworn an oath.'

He nodded at a framed plaque on the wall that said:

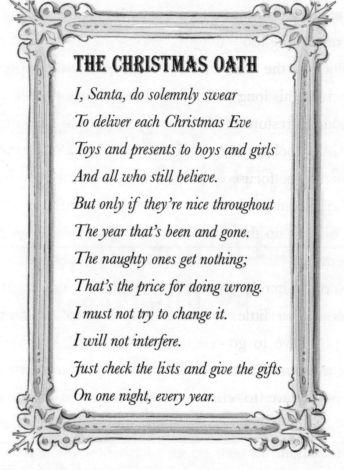

THE CHRISTMAS OATH

I, Santa, do solemnly swear
To deliver each Christmas Eve
Toys and presents to boys and girls
And all who still believe.
But only if they're nice throughout
The year that's been and gone.
The naughty ones get nothing;
That's the price for doing wrong.
I must not try to change it.
I will not interfere.
Just check the lists and give the gifts
On one night, every year.

The Christmasaurus stared intently at the Naughty List, desperately hoping that a way to help William would pop into his head, and wishing that his dino-brain was just a few million years further down the evolutionary chain.

BREAKING RULES

He had the strangest feeling that Santa was thinking the same thing too – not just because he loved William as much as the Christmasaurus did, but also because with a list this long and heavy, a lot of nice needed to be done to restore the balance by Christmas Eve! But, instead of looking at the Naughty List, Santa's wise eyes seemed to be focused on the Christmasaurus. And the dinosaur couldn't help but notice the childlike sparkle that only lit up the old man's face when he was up to something.

'Nope. There's absolutely nothing I can do. It's helpless. *Poor* little William, and all these children, will just have to go without any presents! And we'll have to hope that the balance doesn't tip any further before I have to check the list again *on Christmas Eve!*' Santa bellowed, throwing his arms in the air in frustration.

The Christmasaurus couldn't believe his ears (which weren't really ears at all but small holes hidden away under his icicles). Was Santa really giving up on William, just like that?

'The Naughty List gets longer every year. If we carry

on like this we'll be at one hundred per cent naughty within the next five years.

No more **Nice List**.

No more **Christmas**.

No more . . . **ME!**'

Santa said with a sorrowful frown, pointing to a complicated graph on the wall that showed the troubling upward trend of more names on the Naughty List.

Breaking Rules

'It's no use sitting around scratching our bottoms, trying to think of a way to do the impossible,' Santa said slowly, almost as though he were trying to give the Christmasaurus a chance to really hear what he was saying. 'I can't just scoop up the Naughty List and fly around the world to give these children a little nudge in the Nice direction. I'm Santa – I can't interfere, and I'm so BUSY here with Christmas just a few weeks away.'

Santa marched around the reading room purposefully, every now and then glancing sideways at the Christmasaurus. Meanwhile, the dinosaur wished Santa would be quiet so he could think of how he could save his poor friend from the fate of being a Naughty Lister . . .

Santa abruptly stopped his pacing and turned to face the Christmasaurus. 'Yes, yes, VERY BUSY, which reminds me, I must pop out now for some very important . . . Christmassy . . . Christmas thing . . . and leave the Naughty List *totally unwatched*.' He nodded at the list sitting on his desk. 'If anything were to happen to it while I was gone, I guess I would never know.'

And, with that, he spun on his heels and strode out of the door.

The Christmasaurus glanced at the worrying graph that showed the number of Naughty List names heading dangerously close to **THE END OF CHRISTMAS** line.

Whatever Santa said about it being helpless, there had to be something he could do! His eyes were drawn back to the list, which was just sitting there. Unguarded.

I can't just scoop up the Naughty List . . .

Santa's voice echoed around the Christmasaurus's head. Then he heard it again. Only this time, he forgot a couple of words:

Just scoop up the Naughty List!

The Christmasaurus leapt across the room, grabbing the heavy book of naughty names with his claws like an eagle catching its prey. Then a few more of Santa's words popped into his head:

BREAKING RULES

. . . fly around the world to give these children a little nudge in the Nice direction . . .

. . . It's no use sitting around scratching our bottoms, trying to think of a way to do the impossible . . .

Of course, Santa was absolutely right! *Thinking* of doing something *is* useless! You need to actually *do* something!

This wasn't just about stopping William and all the other kids from having a Christmas without presents. This was about the future of Christmas itself! The balance between naughty and nice had to be corrected, and if Santa wasn't allowed to intervene, then the Christmasaurus was going to have to take matters into his own claws. The world needed Christmas, now more than ever! And, with just twenty-three days to go until Santa's second check of the Naughty List on Christmas Eve, there was no time to waste!

The Christmasaurus launched himself through the open stained-glass window, soaring into the sky with the list held tight in his grip. He was a dinosaur on a mission.

A mission to make the Naughty List nice.

❄

As the Christmasaurus disappeared in a flash of blue, Santa and Buttercream the elf watched from the warm kitchen below.

'What was that, up in the sky?
Something blue went whizzing by!'

Buttercream sang, looking towards the spot in the night sky where the Christmasaurus had just vanished.

'Something blue? I didn't see a thing,' Santa mumbled casually through a mouthful of freshly baked shortbread biscuit.

'Don't pretend you're biscuit-crunching.
Santa, are you up to something?'

Breaking Rules

Buttercream chirped suspiciously, sliding the sugar-dusted biscuits out of Santa's reach.

'Up to something? Me?' Santa said, but he could barely contain his smile as he thought of his trusty blue dinosaur friend flying away from the North Pole on another quest to save Christmas. Hopefully.

CHAPTER FIVE

RONNIE NUTBOG

R onnie Nutbog was tall for his age. In fact, he was about twice as tall as some of his classmates, and he had hands so big that he could hold a basketball in just one of them, which everybody knows is super-cool.

If Ronnie were a superhero, his whopping-great-hands would be his superpower, and if superhero movies have taught us one thing it's that with great power comes great responsibility – and (between you and me) Ronnie Nutbog didn't always use those whopping-great-hands-of-power for good. You see, when those hands were rolled up into fists, they were like two potatoes. And I'm not talking about silly little new potatoes (what's even the point of those?). I'm talking about the ones you use for jacket potatoes – the ones that are the size of your head! Ronnie's jacket-potato-sized fists were quite scary even by themselves, and even more so when they were accompanied by his scrunched-up face grunting:

'Gimme yer lunch money!'

OK, I admit it's not the most original line. In fact, it's been used by bullies ever since cavepeople sent their kids to cave-school – except they used to say:

'GLERF ARGH FLOBBLE CHRUD!'

That roughly translates as 'Give me your firewood!' – and this tactic has stood the test of time because it is still effective, as you are about to see.

Ronnie had always been a bully, ever since his potato fists *were* actually more like new potatoes, but this term he'd got even worse! His school had a tuck shop where the children could buy things like sandwiches and crisps and snacks, and every lunchtime since the summer holiday ended, Ronnie *Potato-fist* Nutbog would stomp towards the small shop, looking for prey. The tuck shop was mostly used by the lower years spending their pocket money on a cheeky little chocolate bar or two, and they queued outside in a nice, neat line along the wall where no teachers could see, making them the perfect targets for Ronnie Nutbog's classic line. OK, here it comes . . .

First, he'd make sure no one was within earshot to hear him deliver those ancient words of terror. Then, once he knew the coast was clear, he'd screw his face up and curl his fists into potatoes before barking:

'Gimme yer lunch money!'

Well, the Year Threes and Fours, who had been eagerly waiting in line for their cheese-and-pickle sandwiches, nearly cheese-and-pickled their pants, and practically threw whatever coins they had at Ronnie's scuffed shoes.

'Take it, you BIG bully!'
they'd cry!

'Just leave us alone!'
they'd tremble!

'Why is he holding POTATOES?'
they'd wonder.

And then they'd scuttle away from the tuck shop with empty pockets and empty tummies, hoping that perhaps tomorrow might be the day that they actually got some tuck!

But when next lunchtime came around . . .

'Gimme yer lunch money!'
Ronnie grumbled.

'B-b-but I'm hungry!' they whined.

'TAKE IT! Just don't hurt us!'
they shuddered.

'He's STILL holding potatoes!'
they noticed.

And in this same way Ronnie had been making his tuck-shop collection nearly every single day during the winter term, which meant that now it was December he'd got quite a hefty sum of money from these little walking cash machines.

It was safe to assume that Ronnie Nutbog was rolling in it. Absolutely minted. He must have had big plans for that money, and all the Year Threes and Fours had their own thoughts about what he had been spending it on, which they loved to discuss with each other in the school's corridors . . .

'I reckon he's spent it on private tuition at Bully School!' said Stephanie Goosens.

'I've heard rumours that he uses our money to buy rare, limited-edition toys online – then he destroys them!' whispered Peter Thompson.

'No way. Have you seen the size of his hands? Those aren't real; they're state-of-the-art robot fists. Only the top bullies in the world have those. Must have cost him an arm and a leg,' said Jack Cooper.

'You mean, a fist and a fist?' corrected his twin brother, James.

But whether it was robot-bully fists, destroying rare collectibles or something else entirely, Ronnie's behaviour was classic Naughty List material, and a certain blue dinosaur was about to get to the bottom of Ronnie's tuck-shop thievery. Which brings us nicely back to that frosty December day when the Christmasaurus was zooming through the sky with the Naughty List in his claws . . .

CHAPTER SIX

NUTBOG'S SAVINGS

T he night rolled on as the Christmasaurus soared
through the sky away from the North Pole, and
soon his icicles glowed with the warm orange
beams of the morning sunshine. Hours passed with the
Christmasaurus's mind focused on one thing: getting his
best friend, William Trundle, off the Naughty List! But
now, as he hovered over a small, unassuming town, the
hefty list in his grip started to feel heavy. Not just a little
heavy; I'm talking Thor's hammer heavy. Fully packed
suitcase heavy. Your tummy after Christmas dinner

HEAVY!

The Christmasaurus glanced down at the book and noticed that a deep purple glow was pulsing from within the pages, as if the Northern Lights were dancing inside and trying to escape.

Suddenly the pages began fluttering about as though someone invisible were flicking through them, and the Christmasaurus struggled to hold on to the frantic book! Then, as quickly as the movement had started, the pages stopped purposely where the purple glow was at its brightest.

The name Ronnie Nutbog glistened out at the Christmasaurus, and a beam of aurora borealis light burst from the letters on the page, shining down like a beacon towards the town below.

The Christmasaurus tried to fly onward, longing to get to William, but the Naughty List was already pulling him

down,

down,

DOWN.

NUTBOG'S SAVINGS

He had no choice but to give in, so the Christmasaurus tucked up his feet and dived like an eagle, following the swirling purple beam straight down through the snow clouds until he came to rest on the roof of a school just as the bell rang for lunch.

The Christmasaurus crouched low and peeped over the edge of the lightly snow-dusted roof.

If the students in the classroom below had known that an actual living, breathing dinosaur was sneaking around just metres above their heads, while they were learning all about the extinction of the dinosaurs, they wouldn't have believed it!

The Christmasaurus did his best to stay out of sight. Luckily his Christmases of pulling Santa's sleigh had made him an expert at hiding on rooftops! It was easy spotting Ronnie, though, and the Christmasaurus watched as the boy approached the tuck-shop queue with his two spud-sized fists balled up, just like the shadow version of Ronnie had done on the Snow Ranch ceiling.

'Gimme yer lunch money!'

Ronnie growled at the younger children in the queue.

The Christmasaurus huffed in disapproval at witnessing someone being so naughty, especially this close to Christmas!

The small kids all obeyed and handed over their money as usual. Ronnie turned and briskly strutted away with pockets full of coins that jangled like sleigh bells as he walked.

Seeing a Naughty Lister at work in real life suddenly filled the Christmasaurus with dino-doubt. How on earth was he ever going to be able to get Ronnie Nutbog on to the Nice List? Maybe he didn't even deserve to move lists. It certainly didn't look like it from where the Christmasaurus was sitting, but if there was one thing he'd learnt from Santa over the years it was that you never leave a mince pie unattended or it will be eaten . . . oh, and also that when it comes to who is naughty or nice, there's often more to it than meets the eye.

The Christmasaurus waited on the roof for the rest of the afternoon, counting the snowflakes he caught on his tongue until the bell finally rang for hometime. Children poured out into the playground, and the Christmasaurus spotted Ronnie creeping away quietly, as though he had somewhere important to be.

The Christmasaurus scooped up the Naughty List and hopped into the air, trying to stay out of sight as he followed Ronnie.

After a few minutes, a bundle of shops appeared on

the road ahead and it became clear that Ronnie was heading towards the high street in the centre of town.

Of course! He's off to buy himself something! thought the Christmasaurus as he perched himself on top of a bus stop across from a parade of shops and watched Ronnie approach the one on the corner. It had a row of bikes in the window and a big sign above the door that read: **WHEELY GOOD**.

There was a huge selection of speedsters and BMXes parked temptingly on the pavement with their metallic paint glistening in the fading winter sun. As Ronnie strolled past them, he ran his fingers over the cool frames, admiring each bike.

Bingo! the Christmasaurus thought.

But Ronnie didn't go inside – in fact, he didn't even pause to look at the prices. He just kept walking, now heading towards **ROCK STOCK**, the drum store.

Ah! What kid doesn't want a drum kit?!

Ronnie did headbang a little at the **booms** and **thuds**

of people trying out the kits inside, but confusingly his eyes didn't flick towards the golden kit in the window that was being blasted with strobe lights and dry ice.

Hmmm, not a musician then, the Christmasaurus puzzled as he watched him continue on his way.

But Ronnie didn't seem tempted by any of the shops he passed.

GIZMANIA, the gadget store? Not bothered.

FREAKY GEEKY, the comic-book shop? Nope, not a flinch.

Sugar Rush, the sweet shop? He didn't even stop for the free marshmallow taster outside.

It looked more and more like Ronnie Nutbog was a kid with a plan. He knew exactly where he was going and didn't stop until he was standing directly outside . . .

ROCKING CHAIR VILLAGE?

Huh? Rocking chairs? The Christmasaurus scrunched up his nose in confusion. He did not see that coming any more than you did.

Ronnie stood at the dusty windows of the beige-coloured furniture shop and stared through the murky glass at a wooden rocking chair with sickly pink fluffy cushions that sat in the window. Ronnie pressed his whopper hands against the glass and looked at the chair as though it were the most precious thing in the world.

After a short while, he peeled himself away from the glass, reached into his pocket and pulled out the stolen coins. He counted how much he had, before disappearing down the next road.

The Christmasaurus followed, trying to piece all this strange information together as he watched Ronnie turn on to **Strike Lane** and head into a house with the number **14** painted on the gate and a broken chimney that looked as though it had been struck by lightning.

'It's only me, Nan!' Ronnie called as the front door clicked shut behind him.

Wanting to see and hear what was happening inside, the Christmasaurus swooshed up to the roof, plonked the Naughty List on the edge of the chimney flue and stuck his head inside, hoping to hear the conversation below. He stretched his neck, leaning into the chimney but, as he did, his clumsy little dinosaur arms nudged the Naughty List and it toppled helplessly into the darkness below.

Well, that was it. There was nothing he could do except close his eyes and go into full Santa mode. That's right. The Christmasaurus went down the chimney.

CHAPTER SEVEN

OLD GRANNY NUTBOG

The Christmasaurus landed with a thud in the fireplace. An ache raced through his mouth as he jarred his wobbly tooth – **OW!** The impact of the small dinosaur's heavy landing forced a cloud of soot into the living room, making it impossible to see anything! But, as the black cloud settled, the Christmasaurus found himself face to face with two potatoes.

Oh, wait, sorry! Those were the two clenched fists of Ronnie Nutbog!

'Get out of my house, you **big** . . .

d -
d -
DINOSAUR!'

Ronnie's mouth fell open like a cod's, and the Christmasaurus gently closed it with his icy claw.

'But . . . you're impossible!' Ronnie gawped. 'Are you going to eat us?'

The Christmasaurus screwed up his face like he'd eaten a mouldy sprout!

Ronnie held up his fists bravely again, but the Christmasaurus nudged them away with his scaly head before looking deep into Ronnie's eyes, which somehow melted away all the bully's worries. It was a little trick he'd picked up from Santa.

'Is that you, Ronnikins?' croaked a voice. The Christmasaurus turned and saw Ronnie's granny sitting on the armchair on the other side of the room, watching TV with the volume up full. Now, Old Granny Nutbog was old. Like, **REALLY old**! She was the kind of old person that you couldn't imagine was ever young and, who knows, maybe she wasn't. Maybe she was born old! But, old or not, Granny Nutbog always had a little twinkle of mischief in her eyes – the same eyes that were now looking straight at the dinosaur in her living room!

'You didn't tell me you got a dog!' she said, squinting.

'Dog?' Ronnie frowned, but the Christmasaurus gave him a nudge and let out his best **WOOF!**

'Dog! Yes, that's right. Erm . . . it's . . . the . . . class pet! I'm just looking after it,' Ronnie lied.

'I see! How lovely. Well, make sure he knows that the Christmas tree is not a toilet, or your parents will make him sleep in the garden!' Granny winked, before turning back to watch her favourite TV show, *Loose Grannies*.

'**Phew!**' Ronnie sighed. 'So, if you're not here to eat us, why is there a dinosaur in my living room?'

The Christmasaurus took a deep breath, preparing himself to break the news that no child on the planet wants to hear. He searched the soot-covered fireplace with his nose like a dog digging for a bone and pulled out the heavy book full of names with his teeth (which he instantly regretted as it wibbled his wobbly one!) and plonked it down with a

thud

at Ronnie's feet.

'What's that?' Ronnie asked.

The Christmasaurus dipped his head and puffed out a gust of air from his nostrils to blow away the soot and reveal the golden letters underneath.

'*The Naughty List,*' Ronnie read aloud, his face turning white. 'Is that the actual one? The real deal?'

The Christmasaurus nodded and, as if by magic, the book fell open and flicked through the pages until Ronnie was staring at his own name.

'Why? That's not fair. I've been on that list before, when I was *proper* naughty, so I know the drill – no presents! But I've not been *that* bad this year! I reckon I've been quite good, *actually*!' Ronnie protested, but the Christmasaurus growled a little and nuzzled the boy's pocket, causing the coins inside to jingle.

'Oh. How do you know about that?' he asked, his face flushing bright red with embarrassment.

The Christmasaurus shook his big, scaly head before tipping it to the side like an inquisitive puppy.

'You want to know why I took the money?' said Ronnie, and the Christmasaurus nodded. 'I . . . I . . . I don't have to tell you!' Ronnie replied defensively.

The Christmasaurus sighed and scooped up the Naughty List before heading to the fireplace as though he were going to leave.

'Wait!' Ronnie's plea stopped the Christmasaurus just before his blue feet were about to disappear up the flue.

Ronnie took a breath and sighed a deep, defeated sigh.

'It all started this summer,' he began, and the Christmasaurus made himself comfy on the floor for story time.

'Mum and Dad were at work – as usual – so it was only me and Granny Nutbog at home. She was sitting in her favourite chair, a rocking chair. That one over there.' Ronnie pointed to an empty rocking chair in the corner that looked almost as old as Granny Nutbog.

'Granny fancied a biscuit and got up to fetch the tin, which is when I decided to leap into her rocking chair – you know, just to give it a go. Those things are awesome! All chairs should rock. Anyway, I was imagining I was a pilot in a jet doing all sorts of ace aerobatics in the living room and as I was about to pull out of a loop-the-loop . . .

CRACK!'

Ronnie clapped his hands together, making the Christmasaurus jump. 'Something must have snapped, and my bottom fell through the bottom of the chair. I guess I rocked the rocking chair too hard and broke it.'

He looked at his feet, ashamed.

'I felt SO bad. It was Granny's favourite chair; she sat in it all day, every day! On top of that, I knew that when my parents found out I was going to be grounded ALL summer! No epic adventures with my friends, and we had big plans! We're in a sort of club – a gang really – called the Danger Gang . . . Wait, I'm not meant to tell people that. Forget I said that, OK?' Ronnie said quickly, and the Christmasaurus mimed zipping his mouth shut with his claw.

'Anyway, I didn't get grounded. Not even told off, because Granny Nutbog DIDN'T TELL ANYONE!' Ronnie said, looking at the old lady like she was his hero. 'I broke the chair good and proper. You can barely sit in it, but, whenever we're all in the living room, Granny pretends everything is normal and perches awkwardly on the edge. Then when Mum and Dad aren't here she shuffles back to the armchair, just so I don't get told off!'

The Christmasaurus thought of the many times that he'd broken pieces of Santa's furniture and suddenly wished he'd had a granny like Old Granny Nutbog to cover for him.

'So,' Ronnie continued, 'I promised Granny Nutbog that I'd fix it, and I did my best. I spent every single day of the summer holiday trying to bend springs back into place and glue bits of wood to wherever they looked like they belonged, but I just couldn't do it. The chair had been rocked for the last time! Then on the way to school on the first day of term I walked past the furniture store in the high street and that's when I saw the **LAZY-GRAN 5000**!' Ronnie whispered, making it sound way more awesome than a rocking chair should.

'The moment I laid my eyes on it I said to myself, *I'm going to buy that for my granny!* The only problem was, my pocket money was nowhere near enough.' He paused and looked down at his pocket, which was heavy with the stolen money.

Ronnie glanced over his shoulder to check that Granny Nutbog wasn't looking, then crept up to an old bookshelf at the far end of the living room. He waved for the Christmasaurus to join him, then he pulled out a shoebox that he had stashed behind a row of books and showed it to the Christmasaurus.

On top of the box there was a label with the words Granny's Chair Fund written in Ronnie's scruffy handwriting, and a photo from a furniture catalogue of the LAZY-GRAN 5000.

He lifted the lid, and it was full to the top with all the pocket money he'd stolen throughout the term.

'I was going to pay them back . . . one day. Somehow.'
Ronnie sighed. 'Honest.'

The Christmasaurus looked Ronnie deep in the eyes,
then glanced back to Old Granny Nutbog. She was sitting
happily in her armchair, chuckling at something one of
the Loose Grannies had said, and the Christmasaurus
made a little sad grumble with his throat.

'The worst thing is that I know Granny would be SO
mad if she knew what I'd done.'

The Christmasaurus let out a small growl.

'OK, not *mad*,' agreed Ronnie. 'She'd be . . . sad.' He
looked at all the pocket money. 'I need to give it all back,
don't I?'

The Christmasaurus nodded a firm *yes*, realizing that
this wasn't about the Naughty List any more. This was
about doing the right thing!

'OK. I'll return it tomorrow, and I know just how!'
Ronnie said with a little smile as he closed the lid of the
shoebox.

CHAPTER EIGHT

BEING NICE

After spending the night curled up like a dog at the foot of Ronnie's bed, the Christmasaurus hid the Naughty List under Ronnie's pillow and walked with him to school. The Christmasaurus barked at other dogs as they passed, fully embracing his role as Ronnie's new 'dog' (although he wasn't sure about the whole 'sniffing other dogs' bottoms' thing, so he gave that a miss).

Ronnie's school bag was so heavy – weighed down by the shoebox full of

coins inside it – that he'd decided to put it on his plastic sledge and pull it to school over the slushy layer of snow that covered the pavements.

'There it is . . .' he said, sighing to himself, as they approached Rocking Chair Village and the **LAZY-GRAN 5000** came into view through the grubby window.

The Christmasaurus had to admit, it did look like a comfy rocking chair – way better than the broken, unsittable one at Ronnie's house. He could certainly imagine Old Granny Nutbog relaxing in such a nice chair,

but it didn't matter what Ronnie had planned to use the money for – stealing is stealing. Even dinosaurs knew that, so the money had to go back.

Sensing Ronnie's sadness at not being able to buy the chair, the Christmasaurus nuzzled his blue nose under Ronnie's big potato-hand and leant on him in a sort of doggy-cuddle.

'Thanks.' Ronnie smiled. 'I'm OK, though. I'm still going to get Granny Nutbog the chair.'

The Christmasaurus bolted upright, breaking his dog act and causing a few passers-by to stare at the strange blue creature in the street.

'Down, boy, there's a good *dog*!' Ronnie said, reminding the dinosaur to play dog. 'I mean, I'm going to work hard and save up all *my own* money. I'll wash the dishes after dinner every night, keep my room tidy – I'll even take the bins out, and those things stink! That should get me some extra pocket money. I'll work super-hard every weekend until Christmas if I have to. Then I'll be able to give Granny the chair, but in the right way.'

The Christmasaurus smiled. Ronnie Nutbog's plan sounded perfect. In fact, it sounded . . . **NICE!**

BEING NICE

They arrived at school and, while Ronnie stashed his sledge with the shoebox behind the bike sheds and then went to his morning lessons, the Christmasaurus scooted up to his hiding place on the roof. He waited there patiently until lunchtime, when the bell rang and a line of kids started to form outside the tuck shop, all looking around nervously, hoping that Ronnie wouldn't show up.

But he did.

'**Oi!**' he barked menacingly, appearing from behind the bike shed. The Christmasaurus sat bolt upright and stared down at the familiar scene. Had Ronnie been lying? That 'oi' certainly didn't sound very 'Nice List' worthy!

'P-p-please, Your Royal Nutbogness, please let us get to the tuck shop today!' pleaded Peter Thompson.

'It's so f-f-f-freezing, and they're serving hot chocolate!' shivered Stephanie Goosens.

'Yeah, and we've only got one pound between us today!' chimed the Cooper twins.

Ronnie stared at them, his face as cold as a block of ice.

The tuck-shop kids knew it was no good. They reached into the itchy pockets of their school-uniform trousers and pulled out their coins.

'Is that all?' Ronnie scoffed.

'It's all we've got!' they protested.

'We'll bring more tomorrow!' Peter offered, not wanting any trouble with Ronnie's potato-fists!

'No, you won't,' said Ronnie. 'Not tomorrow, or the day after or EVER AGAIN!' With that, he pulled the rope of his hidden sledge and sent it sliding towards them over the slippery ground. The lid of the shoebox caught a little wintry breeze and flipped off, revealing ALL their tuck-shop money inside.

'I'm –' Ronnie paused as the stunned queue looked from the shining box of coins to him – 'sorry!' Then he smiled.

The tuck-shop kids were so astounded that they looked as though someone had pressed pause.

'Is this a trick?' asked Stephanie.

'You're having us on, right?' added Peter, gawping at the box of booty.

But Ronnie shook his head.

'No tricks. Just treats,' he said, still smiling, and the tuck-shop kids suddenly burst into a huge cheer as they reached in and took their money back. They danced around in the snow in celebration and thanked Ronnie for returning their pocket money.

'I was trying to do something nice for someone else, but, well, I got it all a bit wrong,' Ronnie explained. 'But it doesn't matter what I wanted the money for. I shouldn't have stolen it from you. It won't happen again, ever. I promise!'

The Christmasaurus watched on, filled with happiness at seeing Ronnie do the right thing.

❄

At the end of the school day, the Christmasaurus was waiting at the school gate, doing his best to blend in with the various dogs that had been brought along by grown-ups doing the school run.

'You're still here?' Ronnie was still beaming, and the Christmasaurus jumped up and licked his face. The action nudged the dinosaur's sore tooth, making it wobble a little in his gums.

'Gross!' Ronnie laughed. 'But, I did it!'

The Christmasaurus angled his head inquisitively, ignoring his aching tooth. This was more important!

'You want to know how it felt?' Ronnie said. His dino-translation skills were getting rather good! 'Well, it felt *nice*!' He grinned and gave the Christmasaurus a pat on the head. 'Now, who wants to go *walkies*?'

The Christmasaurus burst into a run and headed to the park, where he pulled Ronnie up to the top of the tallest, snowiest hill before sending him whizzing down on his sledge.

BEING NICE

They played until the winter sun had almost set and they could barely see each other in the dark.

'It's late! Can I get a lift home?' Ronnie asked, holding up the rope of his sledge for the Christmasaurus to pull.

They shot towards Ronnie's house, with Ronnie sliding about on the high-street pavement, getting a faceful of wet slush that the Christmasaurus kicked up. They skidded around lamp posts, slipped over frozen puddles and zipped past unsuspecting shoppers until . . .

'STOP!' Ronnie yelled.

The Christmasaurus dug his claws in and stopped instantly, causing Ronnie to crash straight into his tail!

The dinosaur whipped round to check that Ronnie was OK, but he was already on his feet, staring at something through the dusty window of Rocking Chair Village.

'Look!' Ronnie cried, pointing at the window display. The **LAZY-GRAN 5000** now had a large sticker on it with one word in big red writing, and that word is the title of the next chapter . . .

Chapter Nine

SOLD!

'Someone else has bought the chair,' Ronnie whispered, barely able to speak with the disappointment.

The Christmasaurus didn't know what to do. It seemed so unfair that this should happen on the same day that Ronnie Nutbog had really tried to turn nice.

Nice?

That gave the Christmasaurus an idea! He grabbed the rope to Ronnie's sledge and bolted down the street, causing Ronnie to stumble backwards on to his bottom and hold on for dear life. The Christmasaurus ran so fast his feet barely touched the floor. In fact, his feet weren't touching the floor – he was flying several centimetres above the ground!

Within a minute they were at Ronnie's house, but the boy had hardly got the front door open before the Christmasaurus pushed past him and dashed up the stairs into Ronnie's bedroom.

'What on earth has got into you?' Ronnie asked, running after the dinosaur. But as soon as Ronnie walked into his room it became quite obvious what the Christmasaurus was up to. He had pulled the Naughty List out from underneath the pillow and was frantically flicking through the pages with his tongue.

He stopped suddenly.

'What is it? Did it work? Am I off the Naughty List?' Ronnie asked, peering through the gaps in the Christmasaurus's icy mane.

Then he saw it too.

'My name's still there.' Ronnie sighed, staring down at his name in golden swirly writing.

The Christmasaurus slumped to the floor, defeated. He had been sure that if Ronnie gave back the money he would move to the Nice List, but it hadn't made any difference at all! How was he ever going to save William, or any other kids on the Naughty List, if he failed at the first one?

'It's OK. You tried your best. I guess it serves me right for being such a rotter in the first place. It's my own fault,' Ronnie said, placing a comforting hand on the Christmasaurus's head. 'It's just not our day today.'

But at that very second, as though the Naughty List had been waiting for the perfect moment in our story, a brilliant golden light started glowing from the page.

Ronnie and the Christmasaurus leapt up just in time to see Ronnie's name fade and vanish from the Naughty List.

They had done it!

The Christmasaurus let out a mighty roar in celebration, and Ronnie started running around with his shirt over his head like he'd scored the winning goal at the World Cup. But their celebrations were cut short by the ding-donging of the doorbell.

'Ronald, there are carollers outside!' Old Granny Nutbog called excitedly up the stairs.

They heard her open the front door and the sound of 'We Wish You a Merry Christmas' came bouncing merrily up to Ronnie's room, as though welcoming him to the **Nice List!**

Ronnie and the Christmasaurus bounded down to the front door, where Old Granny Nutbog stood, happily listening to the festive singers. But, as Ronnie looked outside, he was surprised to see some familiar faces.

'Peter! Stephanie! Jack!' Ronnie grinned at seeing a whole gang of the tuck-shop kids standing in the snow outside his house.

'No, I'm Jack – that's James!' corrected Jack, James's twin.

'Sorry! Nice singing!' Ronnie said.

'Yes, yes, it's delightful!' said Old Granny Nutbog, beaming.

'Well, actually, we're not only carolling,' said Peter.

'Yeah, we're delivering!' chirped Jack and James, and the group stepped aside to reveal a brand-new **LAZY-GRAN 5000**. The very same one from the shop window!

'Merry Christmas!' they said.

'**No . . . way!**' gawped Ronnie.

'You said you needed the money to do something nice for someone, and then we saw this.' Stephanie Goosens pulled out the shoebox that Ronnie had kept the money in, and on the lid was the photo of the LAZY-GRAN 5000 above the words *Granny's Chair Fund*.

'Well, we thought about it and we figured that your gran needed a rocking chair more than we needed chocolate from the tuck shop,' Jack said, smiling.

'But I hadn't saved . . . I mean, *borrowed* enough tuck-shop money for the chair yet. So how did you afford it?' Ronnie whispered.

'When the nice man who owns Rocking Chair Village heard that we were trying to buy the chair for our friend's granny, he gave us a Christmas discount – on one condition . . .' Peter grinned.

'What *condition*?' Ronnic asked with a worried, raised eyebrow.

'That you pay off the rest by cleaning the front window of Rocking Chair Village every Saturday morning!' said Jack.

'We figured that way the chair is from *all of us* – you included! So, we told him you'd love to. Right?' asked James.

Ronnie looked at the tuck-shop gang and at Granny's new chair, and he felt a glow of pride wrap around him like a cosy blanket, knowing that he was going to be able to help too.

'I'm in!' Ronnie beamed, and the tuck-shop gang cheered.

'Oh, you wonderful children!' cried Old Granny Nutbog with tears in her twinkling eyes. It was the nicest thing anyone had ever done for her.

Together, they carried the chair into the warm house and, while they positioned it next to the Christmas tree for Old Granny Nutbog to try, the Christmasaurus crept

quietly up to Ronnie's room.

He picked up the Naughty List in his claws and couldn't help but think that it felt a little lighter now that one of the names inside had vanished. His heart raced at the thought of those scales in the North Pole coming a little closer to being balanced. His work with Ronnie Nutbog was done, and it was time for him to soar into the December sky in search of the next child on the Naughty List – a search that was about to take him to

a kingdom . . .

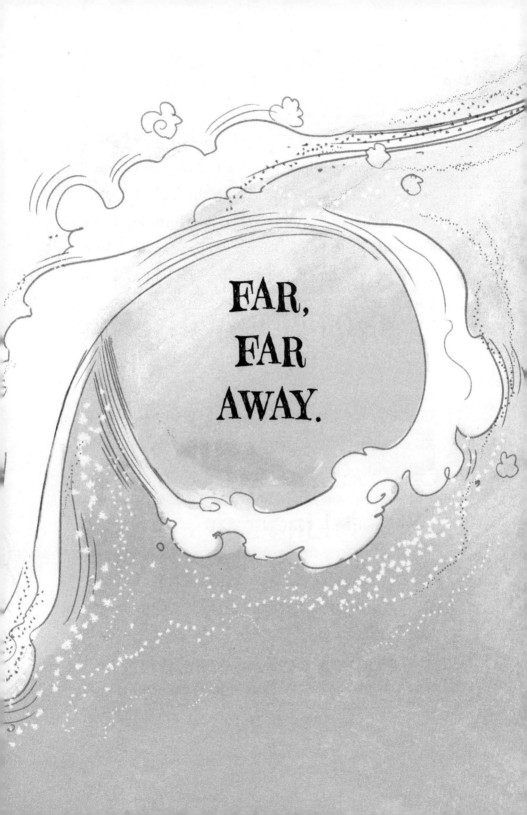

FAR,
FAR
AWAY.

Chapter Ten

TRULY AND UTTERLY SNOTTERSWORTH

In a grand palace, far away from Ronnie and Old Granny Nutbog, lived two truly spoilt and utterly horrid princesses. These twin Royal Highnesses were appropriately named Princess Truly and Princess Utterly Snottersworth.

The princesses lived in a palace that was almost as big as the Queen of England's, with too many bedrooms to count and *forty-three* bathrooms (each with two golden toilets!). The palace also had nine indoor swimming pools, six outdoor swimming pools, a kitchen where a cook made breakfast, a different kitchen where another

cook made lunch and yet another kitchen where both those cooks made supper. There were a thousand televisions dotted throughout the palace, and the princesses demanded that only cartoons were shown on them twenty-four hours a day, even if they weren't home! Should the royal butler, Mr Flimbly, ever try to switch one of the televisions off, Princess Utterly would say:

'I'm the princess and I order you by royal command to turn that television back on.'

Then Princess Truly would chime in:

'Or you'll be thrown in the palace dungeon.'

There was indeed a dungeon in the palace, and I doubt their royal parents would have ever allowed someone to be thrown in it just for switching off a television. But a royal command is a royal command, so the cartoons stayed on.

Now, you might have already decided that Princess Truly and Princess Utterly were truly and utterly spoilt, but you've not even heard the best worst bit yet. Or perhaps it's the worst best bit. I'm not sure – decide for yourself.

In the humongous palace with all those grand rooms and kitchens and golden toilets and swimming pools and televisions, each princess also had their very own playroom.

OK, you might be thinking, *That's not that spoilt! A lot of kids have playrooms or toy-rooms or rooms with toys in*, and you'd be right, but the princesses' playrooms were off-the-scale, record-breaking playrooms.

Princess Truly's playroom was the East Wing of the palace. Not IN the East Wing; it WAS the ENTIRE East Wing.

So that meant, of course, that Princess Utterly's playroom was, as you might have guessed, the

ENTIRE West Wing.

The size of the playrooms meant they were more like mega toyshops – no, toy warehouses! They had every single toy you could ever think of. Seriously. Try it!

Think of a toy . . . Are you thinking of one?

Yep, they had that. In fact, they had three of them. Each.

You want to try again? OK, think of your absolute

favourite toy in the world. The one that you treasure more than any other toy.

Oooh, good choice! And, yep, they had twenty of them. **TWENTY!**

Their playrooms were SO FULL of toys that you couldn't even see the floor, or the walls, or the windows or the ceilings any more. It was just toys, toys, toys, as far as the eye could see, and the only light came in through big glass domes at the top of the rooms.

In fact, the playrooms were crammed with such a lot of toys that the two princesses couldn't even walk around in them. They had to swim! That's right, **SWIM** through the toys.

The palace was so large and the princesses so spoilt that when they wanted to visit their playrooms they would order the royal helicopter, *Snottersforce One*, to give them a lift from the helipad in the fifteenth garden to the helipad on the palace roof. There, each of their personal ponies would be waiting to trot them along the golden roof tiles to the glass domes above their playrooms, where

they would dismount and dive through an opening in the glass panels into the sea of toys below.

Once inside, they would swim about through the sea of teddy bears and dolls, playhouses and trains, remote-control cars and model planes, building blocks and boardgames. It wasn't the most comfortable swimming experience, but the princesses didn't care because knowing that no one else would have a large enough collection of toys to swim through made them very happy.

Did you notice anything unusual about that? Well, I guess it's *all* a little bit unusual (unless you are also a prince or princess with an ocean of toys, in which case, thank you for reading my book, Your Royal Highness). What I mean is, did you spot that the princesses swam about in their toys, but neither of the girls PLAYED with them? They just LOOKED at them as they front-crawled through the superhero shallows into the dollhouse depths, counting their precious possessions with princess-perfect precision.

Why were they counting? I hear you ask.

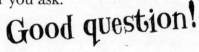

Good question!

They were counting because the one thing Princess Truly wanted was to have more toys than Princess Utterly. And all Princess Utterly longed for was to have more toys than Princess Truly! So, even though they both had what seemed like every toy in the universe, the princesses were in a constant battle to have

more, more, MORE!

And they weren't messing about. In addition to Mr Flimbly's usual royal duties of serving tea, answering calls, serving more tea, greeting guests (with cups of tea), showing guests the way to afternoon tea, and a whole lot of other tea-related tasks, the butler was also ordered to personally count each princess's toy collection. Every day!

This, as you can imagine, was a task that took up most of his time. If you ever visited the palace, you would most likely find him in either the East or West Wing, overseeing his team of royal toy-talliers until supper time, when he served the princesses their dinners before they were washed and dressed for bed, ready for their bedtime story in the bedroom that their parents

INSISTED they share. I mean, they wouldn't want to spoil them or anything!

'. . . and they all lived happily ever after. The end,' Mr Flimbly said one chilly winter's night as he closed the book.

'Well? Who wins today?' asked Princess Truly, as though it had been on the tip of her tongue throughout the entire bedtime story.

'Yes, who is it? Do tell, Mr Flimblypants!' trilled Princess Utterly, making herself and her sister giggle.

'Oh, I think you're both winners, Your Royal Highnesses,' replied Flimblypants . . . sorry, Mr Flimbly, bowing, as he tucked them in.

The giggling stopped instantly.

'Don't be so ridiculous – we can't both be winners. One of us has to have more, and if you don't want to be thrown in the dungeon, it had better be me,' said Princess Truly.

'You? Your playroom looks like an empty cave compared to mine. If I'm not the winner, then it will be ME throwing you in the dungeon!' Princess Utterly snarled, causing Mr Flimbly to have to announce the

actual winner before a royal fight broke out.

'The Princess with the mostess –' he paused to chuckle but was quickly made to continue by their impatient stares – 'is neither of you, as you both have precisely the same amount!' Mr Flimbly revealed, hoping the fact that they were both equal would prevent a royal riot.

'THAT'S NOT FAIR!'

screeched Princess Utterly. 'I'm older, so I should have more! I demand a recount.'

'You're only three minutes older than me,' whined Princess Truly. 'Besides, I'm the smartest so *I* should have more. *I* demand a recount.'

'I shall have the staff count the toys again first thing in the morning,' Mr Flimbly said with a bow.

'Why wait until tomorrow? Make them count them now or throw them all in the dungeon!' demanded Princess Utterly, once again using her favourite empty threat.

'Yes, and I want to visit the toymaker in the town to

get more toys!' said Princess Truly.

'Me too. This is the worst day ever!' Princess Utterly said with a sigh.

Visiting the kingdom's toymaker was a regular trip for the princesses and one you will read about in a few pages.

'Yes, Your Royal Highnesses. We'll put this right tomorrow,' Mr Flimbly said as the princesses both rolled over with a huff in their fluff-tastic beds.

So, while the princesses slept with dreams of even more toys being added to their already toy-riffic collection, the palace staff set to work recounting every building block, ball and stuffed bear. If you had been a bird flying over the palace that night, you would have looked down to see hundreds of busy butlers, giddy guards and frantic footmen dashing back and forth on the rooftop from the East Wing to the West, desperately trying not to lose count.

There wasn't a single bird flying over the palace that night, though. There was, however, a blue dinosaur.

Chapter Eleven

A SECRET GARGOYLE

fter leaving Ronnie Nutbog, the Christmasaurus
felt a tiny jinglewatt of jolliness swirl around in
his tummy due to one name from the Naughty
List being successfully re-listed on to the Nice one.
He was one child closer to restoring the balance of
Christmas, but he knew there was still a lot of work to
be done and not much time to do it in if he was to get
through the list by Christmas Eve. So much, in fact, that
he quickly made a mental, dino to-do list . . .

1. Check that William is OK.

2. Have a snack (being careful with the wobbly tooth, of course!).

3. Save the future of Christmas by helping Naughty List kids become Nice List kids.

4. Have another snack.

5. Double-check that Christmas has been saved.

6. Snack again.

7. Go home and prepare for Christmas Eve . . . while snacking.

As you can see, as well as being a Christmas-saving, loyal best friend, the Christmasaurus was also a keen snacker. Even his

THROBBING,
wobbling,

aching tooth wasn't enough to stop him from thinking about his tummy, BUT right now there were more important things to think about. Except . . . now *I'm* thinking about snacking.

I'd better eat something or this story will end up snack about snack snacky snack-snack too!

Oh, for SNACK'S sake!

Back in a snack . . .

❄

OK, all snacked. That's better. Let's get snack to the story!

As the Christmasaurus soared away from Old Granny Nutbog's house, he closed his crystal-blue eyes, squeezed the Naughty List in his claws and focused on his dear friend William, hoping the list would guide him there next.

But the Naughty List had other plans!

Wisps of purply-red aurora borealis began spiralling from within the pages once again, just like the light that had led to Ronnie. The wisps grew and leapt out into the sky as though they had caught the scent of Naughty Listers nearby.

And they had.

Not just one but two very naughty Naughty Listers!

The swirly lights suddenly twirled themselves into some sort of magical swirly-twirly whirlpool in the sky straight ahead of the Christmasaurus. He couldn't be sure if he flew into it or if the whirlpool sucked him inside, but either way the Christmasaurus went through and found himself in the sky above a grand palace in the middle of a sprawling kingdom just as the sun was starting to rise.

He looked down and saw the ant-like footmen and guards busily darting back and forth on the rooftop, totally oblivious to the extraordinary creature watching them from above. The beams of mysterious Northern

Lights from within the Naughty List's pages floated down to the palace, and the Christmasaurus followed them to an enormous balcony that was surrounded by fearsome stone gargoyles staring down at him.

The doors were closed and heavy velvet curtains were drawn behind grand windows, but as he placed the Naughty List down on the frosted balcony tiles, the pages flicked open to reveal the two glowing names of the rotten princesses who you have already met – Princess Utterly and Princess Truly Snottersworth.

The sun's rays spread across the palace grounds, like someone spreading butter on a crumpet, filling the kingdom with warmth as the birds started singing their morning songs, only to be rudely interrupted by . . .

'I want MORE toys!'

shrieked Princess Utterly from within the bedroom beyond the curtains.

'I want MORE toys!
AND breakfast!'

added Princess Truly, who liked snacking almost as much as the Christmasaurus (and me!).

'Right away, Your Highnesses,' called obedient Mr Flimbly from the rooftop as he hurried the last of the footmen along the golden tiles above.

Suddenly the curtains flew open . . . and the Christmasaurus found himself face to face with a rather unprepared royal maid.

'D-D-D-DINOSAUR!'

she screeched before fainting.

A hundred royal soldiers suddenly stormed into the princesses' bedroom. The Christmasaurus had to think fast or he would be thrown in the dungeon, for sure! He looked around for a place to hide, but all he could see were the eyes of the fearsome gargoyles glaring back at him.

That gave him an idea!

As the soldiers burst out on to the balcony, they found it completely dino-free. They searched high and low, having to shield their eyes from the dazzling morning sunlight, but all that they could see were the fearsome silhouettes of the gargoyles glaring down at them.

'There's no dinosaur here. She must have been scared by the statues!' the soldiers muttered as they marched back inside, and the poor maid went to lie down to recover from the shock. None of them noticed the imposter among the gargoyles: the dinosaur in disguise, the camouflaged Christmasaurus.

From his hiding place, the Christmasaurus saw the princesses bickering and fighting, snatching and stealing from each other's plates, unable to share a single thing as they were served a whopping royal feast of a breakfast in bed that made the Christmasaurus's mouth water.

A Secret Gargoyle

It was torture for the hungry dino with a
toothache to watch the princesses hardly
touch their creamy scrambled eggs on
toast, or the stack of thick pancakes
drizzled with syrup, or the
toasted teacakes, or the sausage
sandwiches, or the bacon baps.
They didn't even so much as nibble on
their two full English breakfasts. It seemed that
every time one of the sisters was given a plate of
something new, the other one lost interest in
the food in front of them and whined
that they were somehow losing out:

'She's got more bacon than me!'

'Well, *she's* got
more syrup on
her pancakes!'

'My apologies, Your
Highnesses,' Mr Flimbly
would reply patiently. 'I'll
make sure that tomorrow, you
each get extra bacon . . .'

'AND syrup!' demanded Princess Truly. 'Just make sure you get it right tomorrow, Flimbly, so we don't have to throw you into the dungeon . . .'

'Yes, of course, extra bacon *and syrup*. Now, as requested the helicopter is ready and waiting to take you to town.' He bowed and left the room.

The twins looked at each other and, in their shared excitement, seemed to agree on something for the first time.

'The toymaker!' they cheered.

This moment of peace didn't last more than a nano-second, though, as it was quickly followed by . . .

'I'm getting more toys than you today.'

'No, *I* am!'

They ran out of the bedroom in a flash, leaving the trays of delicious food abandoned on their beds. The Christmasaurus had a pretty good idea as to why these two young ladies who seemed to have everything were on the Naughty List – having everything wasn't enough!

As the Christmasaurus gazed at the food left behind,

his tummy started to growl as loudly as a helicopter engine. Then he realized that it wasn't his tummy he could hear . . . It actually *was* a helicopter engine! The royal chopper, *Snottersforce One*, was being prepared for take-off, and the princesses were climbing on board.

There was no time to eat now – Christmas was at

stake . . .

steak . . .

steak AND eggs.

The Christmasaurus snapped out of his hungry daydream just in time to see the helicopter zooming away from the palace, and he leapt into the sky after it.*

*He may or may not have quickly slipped a pancake into his mouth first, which made his wobbly tooth hurt but tasted AWESOME!

CHAPTER TWELVE

THE ROYAL TOYMAKER

A s *Snottersforce One* soared over the kingdom, the Christmasaurus followed, desperately trying to think of a way to redirect these two seemingly awful children on to a list that was reserved for nice, kind, caring kids.

The chopper began its descent towards a beautiful snow-covered park surrounded by quaint little shops. Unfortunately, the helicopter created a fierce gust of wind that blasted away all the beautiful snow and freshly built snowmen that the children had spent hours making! Of course, the spoilt princesses inside barely noticed (or cared) that their extravagant method of travel had ruined the snow for everyone else.

A crowd of townsfolk came to the park to see the royal whirlybird land, and, even though they must have been extremely upset by this totally unnecessary and highly inconvenient aircraft ruining their postcard-worthy snow, they all kept perfectly happy smiles on their faces as Princesses Utterly and Truly climbed out of their royal ride.

The townsfolk bowed politely, just as regular, non-royal people do when in the company of royalty, and the princesses waved gracefully, just as royalty do when in the company of everyday people. That was until Princess Utterly and Princess Truly caught sight of the toymaker's shop, at which point they did what neither royal nor non-royal people should ever do and ran, squealing, pushing and shoving one another as they raced to be the first one inside.

'Your Royal Highnesses, what a . . . er . . . pleasant surprise!' the toymaker greeted them nervously as they both fell into his shop (secretly followed by a very fast blue dinosaur who dived into a small pile of stuffed animals).

The toymaker was a kind-looking man with a bushy white beard that reminded the Christmasaurus of Santa's. His eyes were tired, and it was clear from the way he was dressed that he didn't have the time to mend his clothes nor enough money to buy new ones. There were holes in his shoes – you could even see his big left toe sticking out! One of the arms of his glasses had snapped and was held on by some sticky tape. The workshop was also freezing, and as the Christmasaurus looked around he saw a small, unlit fireplace with no sign of any logs or coal to burn.

Compared to the princesses, the toymaker had next to nothing!

Diddly-squat!

In fact, just one golden tile from the palace roof was worth more than the toymaker had made in years! But, despite having no money, he could always afford a smile.

'What have you got for us?' said Princess Truly. 'What's new? Whatever it is, I want two of them. Make that three. In fact, I'll take the lot!'

'I want the most expensive toys. I don't care what they are,' shouted Princess Utterly. 'As long as they're worth a lot of money, I'll take them all!'

'Well, this is a rather unexpected visit, Your Royal Highnesses.' The toymaker gulped. 'Since you were only here yesterday and took every toy from the shop, I'm afraid I've not had time to restock the shelves.'

Princess Utterly and Princess Truly glowered at him with stares so full of naughtiness that for a moment the Christmasaurus actually considered leaving these two firmly on the Naughty List. But then he remembered that this was about the fate of Christmas, and that Santa would say that every child deserved a second chance – even ones that seemed as horrible as these two princesses.

The toymaker's shop wasn't like toyshops you might be used to. Instead it was a real toy workshop where he handmade the most beautiful toys. He could make anything. From model aeroplanes to talking dolls, trains to teddies, cars to castles – he could do it all. Once upon a time, his creations would fill the beautifully carved shelves from floor to ceiling, and the toymaker would zoom around the workshop on one of those ladders on wheels to find the perfect toy for his customers. Getting a toy from his shop was a one-of-a-kind experience and children came from all over the kingdom as a special treat!

Well, that was until the princesses discovered the little toyshop. Unfortunately, their desperate desire to have

more, more, MORE

meant that the poor toymaker could hardly keep up with their impossible toy demands, let alone make enough for all the other children too. The toymaker's workshop had become the personal toyshop for these royal pains and, because they were princesses, they got all the toys they wanted FOR FREE! Of course, this put tremendous strain on the toymaker but he would never,

ever, ever, EVER

deny the princesses any toys for fear of being thrown in the palace dungeon.

So, rather than spreading joy to children across the kingdom, the toymaker's creations were now gathering dust in the princesses' overflowing playrooms, never even being played with. It really was a sad state of affairs.

The only other child who the toymaker had managed to find time to make a toy for was his own daughter, Phoebe. She might not have been actual royalty, but she was more than a princess in her father's eyes and, determined to make her something special for Christmas, he had worked into the early hours of the morning for weeks to carve a beautiful wooden giraffe, her favourite animal. He had finally finished it last night, and was now very glad he had kept it out of sight in his room upstairs.

The Christmasaurus peeped out from his hiding spot and saw that the dusty shelves in this grand-looking shop were mostly empty, other than a few sad-looking toy soldiers, abandoned wheels and loose springs that lay in the shadows.

'You mean, you've got no new toys?' Princess Truly gawped, utterly disappointed at the news.

'So, we've come all this way for nothing?' Princess Utterly whispered, truly shaken by the thought of returning to the palace empty-handed.

'Your Royal Highnesses, I'm beyond sorry, but I'm afraid if I don't sell some toys soon, I shall have to close the shop,' the toymaker confessed, but, seeing the disappointment on the princesses' faces, he sighed and added, 'I'll work overtime to make sure you have something new by tomorrow.'

'Tomorrow? What use is tomorrow?' Princess Utterly sneered.

'When our father hears about this, I would be surprised if he didn't throw you in the –' But before Princess Truly could say *dungeon*, someone appeared in the doorway at the back of the workshop.

'Your Royal Highnesses,' Phoebe said as she bowed.

'Phoebe, what are you doing down here?' the toymaker asked nervously. 'Your Highnesses, this is my daughter.'

'Please forgive my father – he seems to have forgotten that he did make you a new toy.'

Phoebe held out her hand to the twins,

and to her father's astonishment she was holding out the toy giraffe that he had made just for her.

The Christmasaurus thought it was as beautiful as any toy he had ever seen come from the snowfields of the North Pole. It reminded him of Stuffy, the beloved toy dinosaur that had brought him and William together a few Christmases ago.

'Phoebe . . .' The toymaker was about to stop her, but Princess Utterly had already leapt across the toyshop.

'I'll take it!'

Princess Utterly cried as she snatched the giraffe from Phoebe's hand. But no sooner was it hers than her sister had clamped her own greedy mitts on it.

'Where are the others?' snapped Princess Truly, turning towards Phoebe. 'There MUST be others!'

'Oh, I'm afraid that this is a one-of-a-kind giraffe,' Phoebe explained.

'You mean, we'll have to . . .' Princess Truly gasped.

'You want us to . . .' Princess Utterly whispered.

'SHARE?' they shrieked.

The Christmasaurus couldn't believe what his icy blue eyes were witnessing.

'That's right, Your Highnesses,' said Phoebe simply.

And without even saying 'thank you' the princesses left the toymaker's shop, each holding tightly on to one end of the toy giraffe.

The Christmasaurus was about to slip out after them, but stopped as he caught sight of the toymaker crouching down to give his daughter a cuddle.

'Daddy, did you mean it when you said you might have to close the toyshop?' Phoebe asked.

'I'm afraid so, little one. I think that giraffe might have been the final toy this toymaker ever makes.' And, with that, he took off his apron and looked around the barren room, before walking to the door and turning the sign from OPEN to CLOSED.

'Phoebe, that giraffe was going to be your special Christmas present. You didn't need to give it to those two –' He didn't finish his sentence for fear of someone hearing.

Phoebe gave her father a hug. 'I know you were making it for me. It was wonderful, but no toy is worth you being thrown into the palace dungeon. Besides, it might do the princesses good to have to share something.' She smiled, and her words gave the Christmasaurus an idea.

CHAPTER THIRTEEN
ROYAL PASSENGERS

Snottersforce One landed on the helipad on top of the palace and the princesses climbed out awkwardly as both of them tried to keep hold of the giraffe.

'It's going in my playroom first!'

'No, my playroom!'

They bickered on the rooftop like this for twenty minutes while the palace staff watched and slowly lost feeling in their fingers, toes and noses (along with the Christmasaurus, who had caught up with them and was now hiding behind a conveniently low cloud).

'Your Royal Highnesses, your lunch is ready to be served. Might I suggest that you take this wonderful new toy inside and decide later?' Mr Flimbly suggested hopefully. After deep scowls, both princesses agreed.

Things didn't get much better inside the palace. The twins refused to put the wooden giraffe down – each far too worried the other would steal it for themselves and win the battle for the most toys. So they both kept one hand on it at all times while they ate their lunch, which meant that most of their food ended up on the floor (much to the Christmasaurus's delight, as he had sneaked in and was now hiding under the dining table!).

They both refused to let go after lunch too, and they wouldn't even take off their coats and hats after their visit to the toymaker's. They each tugged at the giraffe's beautifully carved ends, trying to take it to their own playroom, until Mr Flimbly suggested they take the toy to their *shared* bedroom to play with *together*.

They held on tight even as they walked through the hallways – not even loosening a finger as they climbed the spiral staircase – and I dare not even think about what they would have done with it if they'd needed the loo! The point is, those two princesses were so determined to keep that toy for themselves that they held on at all costs. The Christmasaurus kept close to them too, watching the whole thing with astonishment through the windows. (He'd decided it was much safer to be back outside!)

'Stop pulling it!'

'I'm not!

Stop trying to steal it from me!'

'I'm not trying to steal it.

YOU ARE!'

'No, YOU ARE!'

As soon as the girls arrived in their bedroom, things soon escalated into an all-out, full-blown, royal tug-of-war.

Princess Truly had hold of the giraffe's head. Princess Utterly had its legs, and they heaved this way, then that way, back and forth while the Christmasaurus watched nervously through the balcony window.

'Let go!'
'No, YOU let go!'

They heaved and pulled, pulled and heaved. Surely someone was going to give in soon? Well, I'm afraid to say that someone *did* give in, but it wasn't either of the princesses . . .

CRACK!

The giraffe's head snapped clean off, sending Princess Truly tumbling backwards before landing on her bottom. Princess Utterly went flying off the bed, and the legs of the giraffe went twirling through the air until . . .

SMASH!

The balcony window shattered as the giraffe's bottom went crashing through it. The princesses scrambled to their feet and ran out to the balcony . . . only to be confronted by a dinosaur!

Princess Truly was about to scream, but her sister quickly put her hand over her mouth to muffle the noise.

The Christmasaurus looked magnificent as the afternoon sun illuminated his icy mane, but the sisters' surprise at discovering a dinosaur on the balcony quickly turned to greed. Princess Utterly removed her hand from her sister's mouth, and they both stared at the impossible creature with selfish eyes.

'I want it as a pet!' cried Utterly.

'I saw it first, it's mine!' insisted Truly.

'Mine!'
'Mine!'
'MINE!'

The Christmasaurus had no choice but to break up the bickering with a ROAR!

'Shhhh!'

Princess Utterly whispered. 'If Mama and Papa come in and see that *Truly* broke a window, she'll be in big trouble.'

'You mean when they see *YOU* broke a window,' Princess Truly replied.

This set them both off arguing again. By now the Christmasaurus was sick of hearing them squabble. Enough was enough! He stomped away and returned moments later with something that was sure to put an end to their bickering.

'*The Naughty List!*' The princesses gasped in unison as they read the golden letters on the heavy book that the Christmasaurus dropped at their feet. The Christmasaurus puffed out through his nostrils, using the air to turn the pages until it reached their glowing names.

'No way! *You're* on the Naughty List!' Princess Truly laughed, pointing at her sister.

'*You are too*, you nitwit,' Princess Utterly said, and they both stared in stunned silence for a moment.

'Truly, do you know what this means?'

'If we're on the Naughty List, then on Christmas Day we get . . .'

'**NO PRESENTS!**' they wailed.

'This is all your fault.'

'No, this is *your* fault!'

Princess Truly turned to face the Christmasaurus with teary eyes and a frowny forehead.

'Listen up, dino. You tell Santa that if he doesn't remove me from the Naughty List, I'll throw him in the dungeon!' she snapped.

'No! If he doesn't remove *ME* from the Naughty List, *I'LL* throw him in the dungeon. And his reindeer too!' Princess Utterly threatened.

'Don't be ridiculous – you can't put reindeer in a dungeon,' her sister argued.

'I can and I will. You just watch!'

'No, *I* will. *You* watch!'

Again, the Christmasaurus stopped the sniping with an almighty

ROOOOAAAAAR

123

that caused the maid who had spotted him earlier to faint in the hallway.

The princesses instantly snapped their squabbling mouths shut. The Christmasaurus carefully stepped over the broken glass on the balcony before bending down to pick something up in his mouth, ignoring the pain from his wobbly tooth as he did so. He placed it next to the Naughty List and the royal twins recognized the broken bottom-half of the giraffe (which now had a little dinosaur drool on it too). Then he picked up the giraffe's head and placed that next to it.

'Big deal, we've got plenty of other toys,' said Princess Utterly, shrugging.

'Yes, it's broken now, so we don't want it. Throw it away,' Princess Truly sneered.

The Christmasaurus growled and nudged the broken toy so that the princesses could see the toy's feet. On the bottom of each hoof (that's right, giraffes have hooves!) there was beautiful writing carved into the wood, a different word on each.

The princesses read out loud together:

124

For Phoebe
Love Daddy

There was a long silence as the twins thought about those words and the broken toy in front of them.

'The toymaker's daughter gave us her own toy?' Princess Utterly asked, and the Christmasaurus nodded. 'Why would she do that?'

'Well, you did say that Papa would throw the toymaker in the dungeon if we didn't get a toy,' Princess Truly said.

'Oh, we both know that isn't true!'

'But, Utterly . . . *they* don't.'

As those words left Truly's lips, both sisters fully realized the power of their silly, empty threats.

'Now that little girl has nothing,' Princess Utterly said sadly.

'Except for what really matters,' Princess Truly added, and looked at her sister.

Suddenly it was as if a light bulb had clicked on in both Truly and Utterly's minds.

'She didn't think twice about giving up the giraffe

for him, even though it was made just for her. Having her dad means more than any toy could,' Princess Truly said.

Their gazes fell to the list next to the broken giraffe where their names glowed a deep gold.

'We have been naughty, haven't we?' confessed Princess Truly.

'I suppose we have,' her twin agreed.

The Christmasaurus nodded in confirmation.

'How can we put this right?' Princess Utterly asked the Christmasaurus, and the icy blue dinosaur couldn't help but smile a little at her question. He crouched low, wagged his tail and let out a little chirp.

'What's it doing?' asked Princess Utterly to her sister.

'I think the strange dinosaur wants us to get on its back.'

'You first.'

'No, you first.'

'No, YOU!'

ROYAL PASSENGERS

The Christmasaurus expelled another impatient chirp and both princesses quickly let go of their fears, climbed on his back and grabbed hold of his icy spines.

In a flash, the Christmasaurus leapt into the sky, carrying the princesses on his back as they soared across the snowy kingdom.

It wasn't long before he dived down low and swooped towards a little house on the outskirts of the town. The Christmasaurus and his royal passengers peered inside to find a room that clearly belonged to a small boy.

'Oh my goodness!' Princess Truly gasped.

'What is it?'

'Look at the toybox!' She pointed at the perfectly normal-sized toybox in the corner of the room, which was open and had hardly any toys inside.

'Oh, the poor boy must be absolutely miserable,' said Princess Utterly. But at that very moment an explosion of laughter came from another room. The Christmasaurus drifted across to the next window. Inside, the boy and his parents were sitting around a small Christmas tree, playing a game where they all had names stuck to their foreheads and were guessing who they were.

'Look, he's not miserable at all!' Princess Truly said in surprise.

'No, he's happy. Very happy! Even though he doesn't have any toys,' Princess Utterly said.

While the princesses thought about that, the Christmasaurus flew on towards a cottage with warm smoke billowing out of the chimney.

They landed in the garden, tiptoed through the crunchy snow to the back door and peered in through the cat flap. At the kitchen table, two children were busily folding up pieces of paper.

'Are you ready?' the boy said.

'Mine is SO going to beat yours,' his sister replied.

The princesses looked at each other.

'See, we're not the only siblings who fight!' whispered Princess Truly to the Christmasaurus, but the dinosaur didn't take his blue eyes off the brother and sister as they leapt up to reveal their paper creations.

'Oh, look, they've made paper aeroplanes!' said Princess Utterly as the children lined up against the kitchen wall. They counted to three, then launched them across the room.

The little girl's aeroplane flew much further than her brother's and she let out a

WHOOP

in celebration.

'Well done, sis! I'll get you next time!' the brother said with a big smile.

Princess Utterly and Princess Truly glanced at each other. These children weren't bickering about cheating or being the best; they were just having fun. And without any fancy toys, either – a simple paper aeroplane was fun enough for them. But, before they had a chance to say anything, the Christmasaurus was off again, galloping across the garden. The princesses ran to catch up and leapt on to his back just as his feet left the ground.

They shot through the streets of the town, catching glimpses of life inside house after house and seeing children who appeared to have nothing compared to the princesses but were full of cheer nonetheless. With each joyful scene they saw, it dawned on the princesses that, while they had everything they could ever dream of, they were actually the most miserable children in all the kingdom.

Finally, the Christmasaurus swooped over the pretty park in the town to his last stop.

'The toymaker's shop!' cheered the girls as the Christmasaurus landed on a crooked rooftop opposite it – but then they saw the sign in the window:

CLOSED PERMANENTLY

'Oh no!' cried Princess Truly.

'This is all our fault,' said Princess Utterly. 'We've been taking all his wonderful toys! The toymaker hasn't had any to sell and he's never charged us a thing!'

They looked at each other and then at the dark, empty shop.

'We don't even play with them,' said Princess Truly, sighing. 'Oh, I don't want a single toy any more!'

'Me neither,' said her sister.

'I want what those other kids had.'

'Yeah, nothing!' said Princess Utterly.

'No – *happiness*,' said Princess Truly, realizing what the Christmasaurus had been trying to show them.

'And someone to share it with,' said Princess Utterly, looking at her sister. Then, for the first time since the Christmasaurus had arrived, he saw the royal twins really smile at each other.

Suddenly Princess Truly stepped on a loose roof tile and slipped on to her bottom! She went sliding down

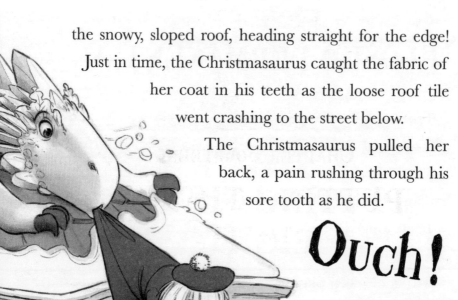

the snowy, sloped roof, heading straight for the edge! Just in time, the Christmasaurus caught the fabric of her coat in his teeth as the loose roof tile went crashing to the street below.

The Christmasaurus pulled her back, a pain rushing through his sore tooth as he did.

Ouch!

'Thanks! That was close!' the princess whispered in relief as she peered over at the red roof tile in the snow. She let out a gasp.

'What is it?' asked Princess Utterly.

'Take us back to the palace!' Princess Truly said to the Christmasaurus before quickly adding, 'Please! I think I know how to put this right!'

Now that was a royal command that the Christmasaurus was more than happy to obey!

CHAPTER FOURTEEN

PUTTING THINGS RIGHT

'**I**'m sorry, Princess Truly,' said a confused Mr Flimbly. 'I must have misheard you. I thought you just said that you want me to load every single toy from your playroom into a giant sack and attach it to *Snottersforce One*, ready to fly immediately!'

'**No!**' said Princess Truly.

'I didn't think so!' replied Mr Flimbly, chuckling.

'I said the toys from *both* our playrooms,' corrected the princess.

'And don't leave a single toy behind!' added Princess Utterly.

Mr Flimbly couldn't believe his ears.

'B-b-but whatever for? It's almost suppertime and then you'll be getting ready for bed.'

'Exactly, and so will all the other children in the kingdom, so there's no time to lose!' Princess Utterly cried.

Mr Flimbly sighed and clapped his hands together, summoning his most-trusted footman.

'Right, you heard Their Royal Highnesses. Every single toy from the playrooms, ready to fly, pronto!' he commanded.

Within seconds the palace was alive with staff, all marching double-speed from the playrooms and through the palace with as many toys as their arms could carry, to an enormous sack made from the royal bedsheets that were being sewn together on the lawn.

The princesses weren't just sitting back and watching this brilliant chaos unfold, though – they were both helping! They each stood among the rapidly shrinking mountain of toys in their playrooms, helping to hand the toys over as staff ran back and forth. They both searched every corner, making sure that no toy was left behind.

As the sun set over the kingdom, the Christmasaurus pranced around giddily on the golden tiles of the palace roof, galloping from one glass dome to the other and peering down at this plan of total *niceness* coming to life.

It soon became clear that one sack, no matter how gigantic, would never be enough to hold all the royal toys, so Mr Flimbly sent for a truck.

When that truck was full, he sent for another.

Then another.

And another.

And by midnight there was one enormous Santa-worthy sack hooked up to *Snottersforce One* and TWENTY-THREE trucks overflowing with the princesses' toys. The pilot fired up the propellers, and the trucks' engines roared into action as the palace staff climbed aboard, ready to go.

'Toys loaded and awaiting your command, Your Royal Highnesses,' Mr Flimbly said as the princesses came running across the garden.

Princess Utterly grinned. 'Thank you. Thank all of you!'

Mr Flimbly opened the door to the chopper and lowered the steps for the princesses to board.

'Actually, we're not flying on that tonight,' said Princess Truly.

'What on earth do you mean, Your Royal Highness?'

And, with that, the princess waved up towards the rooftop and beckoned their new blue friend down.

The Christmasaurus came swooping across the perfectly preened hedges to land between the twins.

The royal guards drew their swords and aimed them at the Christmasaurus, who was now surrounded by the princesses' security.

'Well, pull my cracker, is that a . . .

a . . .

a . . .'

stuttered a stunned Mr Flimbly.

'Dinosaur? YES!'

said Princess Utterly. There was a little **thud** as the maid who had spotted the Christmasaurus first on the balcony fainted for a third time.

'And this dinosaur is our friend, so you had all better lower your weapons,' ordered Princess Truly. The guards did so instantly, with confused and slightly scared glances at one another.

'Now, we'll fly ahead – there are a lot of toys to deliver tonight, so you'll need to keep up and keep quiet!' said Princess Truly.

'Who exactly are we delivering the toys to, Your Royal Highness?' asked Mr Flimbly.

'To the whole kingdom! To every child who has missed out on a toy from the toymaker because of our selfishness. Tonight, we put things right!' said Princess Utterly.

'Are you sure we can do this all in one night?' asked Mr Flimbly.

The Christmasaurus nodded confidently. If Santa could deliver to every kid in the world in one night, then he was sure that if they worked together they could get through all the children in one kingdom! After all, Santa didn't have twenty-three trucks, a whole palace's worth of staff and a helicopter!

'There's just one more thing I need to do before we go,' said Princess Utterly with a little twinkle in her eye, as she and her sister climbed on to the Christmasaurus's icy back. Princess Utterly leant forward and whispered something to the Christmasaurus, who instantly shot into the air and soared up to the golden rooftop.

Mr Flimbly and all the palace staff watched in confusion as the princesses and the dinosaur stood for a moment in the moonlight on the grand, glistening roof, before gliding back down to hover in front of the chopper.

'Right then, FOLLOW US!'

the princesses cried – and, with that, they raced into the cool night.

CHAPTER FIFTEEN

DELIVERING IN THE DARK

The Christmasaurus was in his element. He had spent the last few years at the head of Santa's Magnificently Magical Flying Reindeer and, while this was a far easier job, it was just as important. It was a major toy-delivery operation!

It wasn't long before they approached the first house, the one they'd peered into earlier and seen the boy with a heart full of laughter but an empty toybox. *Snottersforce One* hovered high overhead so the rumbling engine didn't wake the sleeping townsfolk below, then the Christmasaurus flew Princess Utterly and Princess Truly up to the overflowing sack of toys that was suspended beneath.

They reached in and pulled out a big model dinosaur, which made the Christmasaurus roar with approval, before he dived down so the twins could place their gift on the doorstep.

The first present had been delivered and so, with a nod of her head, Princess Utterly gave Mr Flimbly the go-ahead to let the delivering commence.

The palace staff set to work, grabbing toys from the trucks and carefully placing them at the homes of children throughout the town. They slid smaller gifts through letterboxes, slipped slim toys through cracks in open windows and left whopping great big ones on doorsteps!

'Wow, who'd have thought that giving something to someone else feels so much better than getting something yourself?' said Princess Truly, beaming, as she looked down and saw their team dashing from house to house with arms full of gifts. It made happy little bubbles float about in her tummy.

Princess Utterly grinned. 'It does, doesn't it?'

But there wasn't time to stop and enjoy the feeling just yet – there was still a lot to be done! So they were off in a flash, racing from house to cottage, from doorway to windowsill, postbox to plant pot, leaving toys and gifts of all kinds for the children of the surrounding villages and towns. Meanwhile, the palace staff continued up and down every side street, cul-de-sac, mews, lane and avenue, showering their residents with toys. With every street they visited, the overflowing sack of toys seemed to deflate like a balloon the day after a birthday party.

It was exhausting work – as you can imagine – but no one gave up, and it wasn't until moments before sunrise that the last of the toys was delivered.

The palace staff gave a very, **VERY** quiet cheer so as to not wake anyone up.

'Congratulations, Your Royal Highnesses. You have successfully given every single one of your toys to the children of the kingdom. Now, let's get back to the palace before they wake up!' suggested Mr Flimbly.

'Actually, we've still got one more gift to deliver. We'll meet you back at home,' Princess Utterly said, smiling.

'Very well,' said Mr Flimbly, signalling for the

helicopter to head home as he himself leapt on to the back of one of the twenty-three now-empty trucks.

Princess Utterly and Princess Truly climbed on to the Christmasaurus's scaly back again.

'Last stop, the toymaker's shop,' said Princess Utterly.

The Christmasaurus sped off in a blur of blue, landing on the cobblestones outside the toymaker's shop barely a minute later.

They looked again at the sad sign on the door.

CLOSED PERMANENTLY

'Not if we have anything to do with it!' said Princess Utterly. She reached into her pocket and pulled out something heavy that she'd been hiding under her dressing gown.

Truly smiled as she looked at the object in her sister's hands. The morning sun was beginning to make its way across the town square, and the twins' faces glowed with a golden warmth, although the Christmasaurus thought that it was probably more than the glow of the sun that was making the twins seem to shine. It was the joy they had found in giving.

A light flickered on inside the toymaker's workshop – he was awake!

Quickly, Princess Utterly placed their final gift on the doorstep and tapped her knuckles loudly on the thin glass –

TAP!

TAP!

TAP!

Then the princesses leapt on to the Christmasaurus's back and he flew once more up to the opposite rooftop, crouching out of sight as the shop door opened.

'Hello?' the toymaker called, looking up and down the seemingly empty street. Then his eyes fell on something at his feet.

Something SHINY.

Something GOLD!

'What in the world . . .?' he said, picking up the smooth, shining slab of gold that the princesses had left at his door.

'What is it, Daddy?' called little Phoebe from inside the workshop, but the toymaker was too stunned to answer, so his daughter came to see for herself.

'Is that –'

'Solid gold!' whispered the toymaker in shock.

'But where did it come from?' Phoebe asked.

'I haven't a clue!' her father replied, turning the valuable metal over in his hand to reveal a piece of paper stuck to the other side.

'It's a note! What does it say?' cried Phoebe with excitement, and so the toymaker read it to her:

To the toymaker,

We are very sorry for taking all the toys.
We realize now that the other children in
the kingdom deserve them more than we do,
and we hope this golden roof tile will repay
you for all the toys you have given us. It is
our dearest wish for you to reopen your shop
and continue to make wonderful toys for all
of us to enjoy.

We hope you will let us come back again,
and we promise to only pick ONE toy.

Yours royally,
Princess Utterly and Princess Truly.

PS We're very sorry but we broke the giraffe.
Please thank Phoebe for giving it to us, and
we hope you can make her a new one.

'How curious,' the toymaker said. 'I wonder what happened to the princesses to make them change their ways?'

'Does this mean you'll reopen the toyshop?' asked Phoebe hopefully.

'Yes! Yes! Yes! Now I can make toys for everyone!' the toymaker cheered, lifting Phoebe way up into the air with the biggest smile on his face.

As the toymaker and his daughter took their glistening gift into the workshop, the Christmasaurus and the princesses floated on a cloud of happiness back to the palace.

They landed on the balcony and the girls skipped inside their bedroom, giggling with giddiness.

'That was the best night EVER!'

the twins cried.

The Christmasaurus was full of wondrous joy too. Delivering toys to children had become his life's work, and he usually only got to do it one night a year, so he felt very lucky to have been able to help in sharing the toys tonight too. But there was a reason for this extra delivery, and he was eager to see if it had worked.

He ran straight to the Naughty List and nudged it open with his scaly snout.

'Did it work?' asked Princess Truly.

'Are we still naughty?' added Princess Utterly.

Peering through the gaps in the Christmasaurus's icy mane, they saw their names fade into nothing on the page.

'WE'RE NICE!'

the princesses cheered, and hugged each other.

The Christmasaurus, however, wanted to make sure that these two royal sisters remembered the lesson they had learnt that night, and to never forget the happiness they had found in sharing rather than being selfish.

He spotted the two halves of the giraffe lying on the floor and had an idea.

He scooped up the legs and stood them on the princesses' dresser, before carefully picking up the head and balancing it on top.

'That won't do – any little breeze from the balcony will knock that head right off again,' said Truly.

'Hang on!' Utterly cried, as she dived into one of the drawers of her dresser. She pulled out her pencil case and found a glue stick.

'Great idea!' said her sister, smiling as she picked up the giraffe's head and held it steady for Utterly to cover the broken end with a big dollop of glue.

The Christmasaurus couldn't hold back the big

149

toothy grin that had spread across his face; even his wobbly tooth was joining in the smile at the sight of the princesses working together.

They carefully placed the giraffe's head back on the body and, now that the two halves were together, it stood tall and powerful, just like the princesses.

'We'll share him,' said Princess Truly softly, realizing what the Christmasaurus was trying to say.

'And we won't let him break again,' promised Princess Utterly. Together, they wrapped their arms around the Christmasaurus in thanks.

Suddenly the pages on the Naughty List began flapping, then settled on a new page that sent a blast of purple wispy light beaming out through the open balcony doors.

The Christmasaurus bowed to the princesses, and they gave a little curtsy in return as the Naughty List rose into the air and zoomed towards the balcony as if it had a mind of its own.

There wasn't a second to lose if the Christmasaurus wanted to keep up with the Naughty List and restore the balance between naughty and nice before

Christmas Eve. He galloped across the bedroom and raced after it as the heavy book took to the sky, leading the Christmasaurus towards the rising sun and on to the next name on the Naughty List.

CHAPTER SIXTEEN

GAMERKIDD3000

From twin sisters to a big brother, meet GamerKidd3000.

OK, that isn't his real name (although that would be pretty cool). His real name is Marvin Johnson, and he used to be the best big brother in the world to little Braydon.

Marvin was three when Braydon was born, and from day one he took his big brother duties very seriously.

Marvin taught his little brother everything he knew, helping him to crawl and then walk – and how to climb and run!

And, as they grew up, they realized that they weren't just brothers. They were best mates too! Wherever Marvin went, Braydon was usually just behind him, and they did absolutely everything together.

First it was skateboarding. They both got boards in their favourite colours – Marvin's was red, and Braydon's was blue. They spent one whole summer tearing up the street and trying to ollie the curb.

Then it was football. They both started supporting their local team, Trumpton City, and even got matching kits with their favourite player Harry Walker's number on the back.

But what Marvin loved most of all was

PING-PONG!

And he waited impatiently for Braydon to grow up (literally!) so that he would be tall enough to see over the table, and he could finally teach his little brother how to play the best game in the world!

Ping-pong was a Johnson family tradition and

Marvin loved playing ping-pong with his dad. They had a table in the garage so they could play any time they wanted. Morning. Afternoon. Night. Rainy days when the garage flooded and they had to play in wellies; snowy days when they played in their winter coats and mittens; and even days it was so hot that they had to keep the garage door open and just wear their underpants!

Any time was a good time to play ping-pong!

Which is why Marvin was so excited for the day when his little brother was finally big enough to play ping-pong too! Braydon was a quick learner and was soon just as good as his brother, meaning they got into some serious ping-pong battles!

'Let's play a doubles challenge!' their dad said one day when Uncle Lee had come round to visit. 'Brothers against brothers!'

'Great idea!' said Uncle Lee. 'Now, you two need to have a team name if you want to play together,' he said, pulling out a chalkboard to capture the scores.

'A team name?' said Marvin.

'Yeah, when your uncle and I used to compete we were known as . . . **THE KING PINGS!**'

their dad roared triumphantly as he and Uncle Lee struck a hero pose.

'That's so lame,' Braydon said, laughing.

'Well, if you don't want to think of a name, then we'll come up with one for you,' their dad said with a mischievous smirk as he started writing something on the chalkboard.

'Today's game is the King Pings versus

THE PONGERS!'

Uncle Lee hooted with laughter.

'The Pongers?' Marvin screwed up his face.

'Yeah, because you two stink so bad!' Dad teased.

'Oh, really? Well, we'll see who stinks when the Pongers beat you!' Braydon challenged.

'It's on like ping-pong!' Their dad grinned as he served the first ball.

Now, you might think that the grown-ups would have wiped the floor with the kids, but Marvin and Braydon discovered something momentous that day. They realized that, however good they were when they played *against* each other, they were ten times better when they were *on the same team.* It was like the Power Rangers forming Megazord, or the Avengers assembling or when the Christmasaurus first met William Trundle; only instead of saving the world they were hitting a tiny ball back and forth with a paddle . . . But, still, Marvin and Braydon were **AWESOME** together!

From that game on, Marvin and Braydon *only* played doubles. They even had their own team motto:

Two brothers, ONE TEAM!

It didn't take long for them to become the best ping-pong doubles team in the entire school. Fine, they were the *only* ping-pong doubles team in the entire school, but they were still really super good at it. So good, in fact, that their PE teacher, Mr Bench, entered them into the . . .

JUNIOR PING-PONG CHAMPIONSHIP!

The tournament happened every December, and the best ping-pong teams from schools around the whole country came together to compete!

Now, if this were a made-up story, like in the movies, then Marvin and Braydon would have totally smashed all the other teams to win first place at the tournament, been carried out of the championship on the shoulders of all their school friends and gone down in history as ping-pong legends with sponsorship deals coming out of their eyeballs, touring the globe on their private jet and living happily ever after.

But this is real life, so none of that happened.

Instead they were wiped out of the Junior Ping-Pong Championship in the final by another team of brothers called Percy and Paul Paddle, aka the Paddle Bros from Ping-Pong Prep School (I know, you couldn't make it up!).

The game wasn't even a close match. The Paddle Bros

made beating them look as easy as eating pizza (yes, that's a saying!). Seriously, those Paddle Bros moved so fast it looked like they had four extra arms attached to their forearms.

One of them even returned a serve while doing a one-handed backflip using his brother's head as a springboard. I mean, technically that was an illegal move, but the referee thought it was so awesome that they let it pass.

Up until that moment, Marvin and Braydon had never played anyone better than them. And, even though coming second was still pretty amazing, as Marvin and Braydon watched the Paddle Bros leave the championship to roars of applause, they made a promise to each other:

'Next year, that trophy is ours!' Marvin said. 'We're going to practise hard and WIN!'

'Deal!' Braydon said, putting out his hand.

'Two brothers, one team . . .
ONE DREAM!'

they chanted together, and shook hands.

When they got home that night, they stuck a photo of the trophy on the garage wall so they could see it whenever they practised. That was the goal. That was the dream. Together they would make it happen.

Here's where it all went wrong.

CHAPTER SEVENTEEN

WHERE IT ALL WENT PONG

That Christmas, Marvin asked for THE hottest toy that every other kid in his class was asking for: a GameBox. The brand-new handheld video-game console that was *the* must-have present.

Marvin had never really been that into video games before, but this one looked super-amazing. It had a 4K3D SUPER-MEGAPIXEL screen that was so sharp it was supposed to look more real than real life. The sound was ear-drum-blastingly loud, and it had face-recognition, motion-tracking, augmented reality and about a billion other things that I'm too old to even know what they mean, but YOU would have totally loved them.

As with everything else, Braydon had wanted to be just like his brother, and had asked for a GameBox too. But, being three years younger than Marvin, his parents thought he wasn't old enough. Braydon didn't really mind, though, especially as he got a new set of ping-pong balls and an awesome new paddle instead.

'Fancy a quick game before the turkey's ready?' Braydon asked his brother, spinning his new ping-pong paddle around in his palm.

There was no reply.

'Marv?'

Still nothing.

'Hey, Gamer-kid!' Braydon teased, batting a ping-pong ball across the room so it gently bounced off his brother's head.

'Oi! I'm trying to set this thing up!' Marvin snapped.

'I don't have time for a game now, Braydon!'

Braydon burst out laughing. Marvin never said no to ping-pong.

'Good one, bro! Come on – we don't have long until Christmas dinner.'

'I'm serious, Braydon. Maybe later,' Marvin said, not even looking up from the gleaming screen.

Braydon was stunned. He'd never had to play without his big brother before. As he trundled out of the living room towards the garage, Marvin called out to him.

'Hey, Braydon?'

He came running back, hoping his brother had changed his mind.

'What did you call me a minute ago?' Marvin asked.

'Gamer-kid? It was just a joke – I didn't mean . . .'

'That's perfect!' Marvin grinned, and he started typing it into his new device.

'You can now call me GamerKidd3000!' he announced triumphantly.

Braydon laughed so hard that he snorted like a pig.

'Hey, it's my gamer tag,' Marvin said, annoyed.

'So you're a *gamer* now, are you?'

'I will be! This GameBox is so cool, but you wouldn't understand because you're too little!'

'Marvin! Braydon! Dinner's ready!' their mum shouted, breaking up the argument.

'It's not Marvin any more, Mum,' Braydon teased. 'He's called Gamer*Dork*500.'

'It's Gamer*Kidd3000*!' Marvin snapped.

Things went from bad to worse as Marvin didn't say a word to Braydon over Christmas dinner. Not because he was still mad at him for calling him GamerDork500, but because his face was glued to his brand-new toy. The screen was just so vivid and sharp that the graphics were almost hypnotizing!

'Marvin, aren't you going to eat something?' his dad asked.

'Not hungry,' Marvin mumbled.

'Pull a Christmas cracker then?' said Braydon.

'Oh, if I have to!' he moaned, quickly taking one hand off the controller to feebly hold one end of a cracker while Braydon pulled the other, never taking his eyes off the screen the whole time.

'Well, I'm glad you like your new toy, kiddo!' Dad

laughed, letting him get away with it because it was Christmas.

But Marvin didn't look up for the rest of Christmas Day . . .

When the flaming Christmas pudding came out, Marvin was looking at the screen.

When the family played party games around the fire, Marvin was looking at the screen.

When they sang carols at the piano, Marvin was – you guessed it – looking at the screen!

He even managed to put on his pyjamas *and* brush his teeth without taking his eyeballs off that

dazzling,

hypnotizing,

4K3D SUPER-MEGAPIXEL SCREEN.

But Christmas Day was only just the beginning.

Marvin hardly came out of his bedroom for the rest of the Christmas holidays! He sat in there, his curtains closed, playing video games for hours.

'It's snowing!' Braydon called one morning.

'*Merhm merph,*' Marvin mumbled from behind the screen in the depths of his room.

'*Do you wanna build a . . .*'

But the door slammed in Braydon's face before he could finish the song. You might be thinking, *So what if Marvin skipped building snowmen in the park? He just wanted to enjoy his new toy. Give the kid a break!* But it didn't stop there. The snow day wasn't the only thing he missed . . .

Where It All Went Pong

When Uncle Lee got married to Auntie Giorgina in February, Marvin sat at the back of the church with his face glued to *Footie Frenzy*, the football game where he was playing as his team, Trumpton City, and it was a penalty shoot-out.

He had got so good at hiding his gaming from his parents that no one even knew he'd sneaked the GameBox into the service until the vicar said:

'If any person present knows of any lawful impediment why these two people may not be joined in marriage, he or she should declare it now . . .'

Which happened to be just when Marvin scored the winning penalty as his favourite player, Harry Walker.

'GOOOOOAAAAAAL!'

he yelled, and it echoed around the cavernous church for what felt like ten minutes.

And it still didn't stop there. The whole family went on a sightseeing holiday to Paris during the Easter holidays. Braydon saw everything there was to see in the city; Marvin played CITY-CRAFT on the GameBox.

They went to the cinema to watch the latest superhero movie, and Marvin played *SUPER KID* on the GameBox!

They went to the seaside in the summer, and Marvin ended up with tan lines in the shape of the GameBox on his chest because all he did was play **SURF CHAMPION** while his brother actually surfed!

Marvin even skipped his own birthday party, staying in his bedroom playing **SKATEPARK RAIDERS**, the new skateboarding video game, while his school friends ate his cake and skateboarded *for real* in the garden.

But there was one thing worse than ALL those things put together.

Marvin STOPPED playing PING-PONG with Braydon.

WHERE IT ALL WENT PONG

'Come on – just one game! We need to practise if we're going to win the Junior Ping-Pong Championship. It's only a few weeks away now!' Braydon begged into the darkness of Marvin's room.

'Can't. Gaming,' Marvin barked like a zombie.

That was it. Braydon snapped. He flicked the light on, causing Marvin to cower under the bedcovers like a vampire in daylight.

'What are you doing?!' Marvin whined.

'Hi, Gamer*Dork500*, I'm looking for my brother, Marvin. Is he in there?'

'For the millionth time, it's GamerKidd3000, and you just made me lose the game!'

'Whatever, Marv! We made a deal last year. Remember? We're going to beat the Paddle Bros and win that trophy!'

'I don't care about a stupid trophy. I'm winning all the trophies and medals I need right here!' Marvin snapped, waving his GameBox at Braydon. 'That's more important than winning a pointless chunk of metal to gather dust on the shelf.'

Braydon couldn't believe his ears.

'But you promised.
It's two brothers, one team,
NOT
one brother, ONE SCREEN!'

he shouted, but then he heard the music of Marvin's GameBox start up from underneath the covers. Braydon tore them back to find Marvin's face once more glued to the screen and, worst of all, he was playing a ping-pong video game!

'I don't care about the stupid trophy any more. Don't you get it? I'm a gamer now. As in, VIDEO games. Real ping-pong is as BORING as you are! Now leave me alone!' Marvin said, not even looking up at his brother.

And, just like that, Marvin was on the Naughty List.

CHAPTER EIGHTEEN

FEELING SO LOW, FLYING SOLO

The Naughty List was speeding through the sky as the Christmasaurus raced to keep up. The big book seemed to have a mind of its own, staying just out of biting distance and meaning the Christmasaurus had no choice but to follow.

Beneath him, snow-covered fields and villages turned into towns, which turned into cities, until finally the Naughty List began to slow as it found the home of Marvin and Braydon Johnson, and came to rest on their garage roof with a dull, snowy thud.

The Christmasaurus pounced on the list as though it might escape again, but it didn't put up a fight. Instead it just released a beam of light in the direction of the bedroom window facing him.

A cool blue glow lit up the room from within, and when the Christmasaurus crept towards it he caught sight of the silhouette of a boy with his nose practically touching a video-game screen.

'Marvin, breakfast is on the table!' someone called from the kitchen, but the boy, Marvin, didn't even look up.

Eager to see the rest of the family, the Christmasaurus quietly flew down to the back garden to take a peek through the kitchen window. He saw Mrs Johnson making bacon sandwiches (which was a little distracting for a snack-obsessed dino!) while Mr Johnson brewed a pot of coffee. Then a strange sound caught the Christmasaurus's ear – a gentle

tap . . .

tap . . .

tapping.

Actually, it *wasn't* tapping. It was more like a faint

Ping ... *Ping* ... *ping*

coming from inside the garage.

A small door that led to the garage from the garden patio was slightly ajar, and the Christmasaurus softly slid his snout through the crack to investigate further. Inside he saw a small boy hitting balls across a ping-pong table.

Ping!

He served the ball perfectly, and it shot across the net and landed in the washing basket.

'Braydon, breakfast!' his mum called from the kitchen.

'Coming, Mum,' the boy replied, but the Christmasaurus could sense a clear sadness as he put the paddle down and glanced up at the photo of a golden trophy that was stuck on the garage wall.

The Christmasaurus had to dive behind a huge plant pot to avoid being spotted as Braydon left the garage and jogged across the snowy patio and in through the back door of the house. Then the Christmasaurus quickly zipped back to the kitchen window to listen some more. Why had the Naughty List brought him here?

'How's my boy feeling about the championship today?' his dad asked Braydon.

Braydon just sighed.

'Oh, don't be like that, honey. You'll do just fine on your own,' his mum said encouragingly.

'I'm a doubles player, Mum, and I've lost my double!

Feeling So Low, Flying Solo

I'm like ping without the pong!' he said, pushing his bacon sandwich away.

Marvin appeared at the kitchen doorway, still gripping his console and staring at the screen. He grabbed a bacon sandwich with one hand, put it in his teeth and carried it out of the room like a dog carrying a bone, not looking up once.

Braydon sighed as he watched his brother disappear.

'See, Marvin doesn't even remember it's the championship today! What you don't get, Mum, is that the really fun part of ping-pong was playing with –' The clock on the kitchen wall chimed ten o'clock, stopping Braydon from finishing what he was going to say.

'Is that the time? I'd better get to work! I'll see you at the competition this afternoon. I know you'll pong!' Mum smiled. 'Wait, I don't mean *pong* like smell – I meant, like, ping-pong!'

'I get it, Mum. Actually, can you give me a lift?' Braydon said as he stood up, having not touched his breakfast.

'Sure, but isn't it a bit early?' she asked.

'I thought I'd go and check out the competition.

See who's going to beat me today,' Braydon said, stuffing his ping-pong paddle into his bag.

'Good luck!' called his dad as Braydon followed his mum to the front door.

'Hey, GamerKidd3000!' Braydon called up to his big brother just before he turned to leave the house. 'If you change your mind, registration to enter the doubles tournament closes at two o'clock. I'll be there. Two brothers, one team . . .'

But there was no reply.

Braydon shook his head, shrugged on his coat and headed out of the front door.

The Christmasaurus now knew exactly why the Naughty List had brought him here. Marvin seemed to ignore anything that wasn't happening on his console's screen, and had even stopped thinking about how his brother might be feeling.

An idea went

PING

in the Christmasaurus's mind. He knew what his mission was: to turn GamerKidd3000 back into Marvin and get him to that championship before the two o'clock registration.

The countdown had started!

CHAPTER NINETEEN

CHRISTMASAURUS3000

The moment Mrs Johnson left for work, Mr Johnson placed a shiny black vinyl on an old-fashioned record player, which reminded the Christmasaurus of the great gramophone Santa used to make the sleigh fly on Christmas Eve. Mr Johnson started shredding a sick solo on his air guitar to an invisible crowd in between clearing away breakfast, completely unaware of the very still Christmasaurus behind the plant pot. A few moments later he carried a recycling bag outside and disappeared down the side of the house, leaving the back door open!

CHRISTMASAURUS3000

The Christmasaurus didn't waste any time. He darted inside and charged upstairs, straight into Marvin's bedroom, which was so untidy that the Christmasaurus caught his claws on an old pair of jeans that were lying on the floor and came down with an almighty crash. He tumbled across the carpet, knocking over a laundry bin and sending smelly pants and stinking socks up into the air, before finally landing face-first in what was left of Marvin's bacon sandwich.

Usually crash-landing into food would be a dream come true for the Christmasaurus, but not today. Firstly, hitting the floor caused his wobbly tooth to wobble *even more* and throb with pain – **OW!** Secondly, knowing that most humans' reaction when coming face to face with something extinct was to scream or run away (or both), he had hoped for a slightly less dramatic entrance when he met Marvin.

The Christmasaurus leapt up, heart racing, ready to face a terrified Marvin – but, to the dino's surprise, the boy didn't do anything. In fact, he was so engrossed in his GameBox that he hadn't even noticed that a dinosaur had just exploded into his bedroom!

'Braydon, I thought I told you to knock when you want to come into my room!' Marvin grumbled, not lifting his eyes from the flickering screen.

The Christmasaurus looked around at the dusty posters on the walls: Marvin's favourite footballer, Harry Walker, scoring a goal while wearing a glistening red-and-white stripy Trumpton City kit; a skateboarder soaring high into the air; and the oldest and dustiest poster showed the ping-pong world champion lifting his golden paddle-shaped trophy in the air in celebration as adoring crowds cheered in the background. All the things that Marvin used to love before he'd got lost in the GameBox.

'If you've come to try to convince me to play, then you're wasting your time, lil' bro,' Marvin said, smirking.

The Christmasaurus had had enough. He let out a low but very definite growl through his teeth.

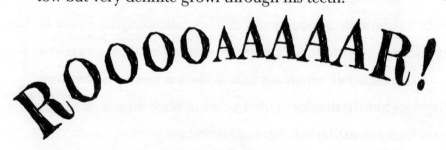

ROOOOAAAAAR!

The noise was so loud it blew back the hood that had been covering Marvin's head and even sent a dollop of dino drool slopping over the screen of his GameBox.

'AHHHHHHHH!'

Marvin squealed. 'Dad! There's a *giant lizard* in my room!' But Marvin's dad couldn't hear a thing because of the sweet heavy-metal riffs he was blasting out in the kitchen. He hadn't even heard the Christmasaurus's deafening roar rattle every coffee mug in the cupboard!

Marvin was on his own as a rather cross-looking Christmasaurus stalked towards him, ice-cold eyes fixed on the glowing device in Marvin's hand.

'This? You want my GameBox? I'm about to come first place in **SKATEPARK RAIDERS**! Do you know how hard that is?' Marvin protested, showing the Christmasaurus the paused skateboarder on the screen.

Marvin was obsessed! There was only one thing for it. The Christmasaurus suddenly grabbed the GameBox in his teeth, then shot straight out of Marvin's bedroom.

'Hey!' Marvin spang up from the Marvin-shaped crater he'd left in his mattress and chased after the thief. He followed in hot pursuit as the Christmasaurus scuttled across the hallway, down the stairs and out of the front door. In his desperation to get his most-prized possession back, Marvin followed and was only shaken to his senses when his bare toes hit the freezing paving slabs outside.

BRRRRᴿRRR!

But Marvin wasn't giving up without a fight. As the icy-blue bandit raced off down the street, Marvin looked around and spotted something hidden under a pile of shoes back in the hallway – his skateboard! He dragged it out, threw on some trainers and leapt on. Then, for the first time in a year, he zoomed off in pursuit.

Marvin was definitely a little rusty, but he soon found his rhythm as he shot across the icy pavement, feeling the wheels glide over the smooth surface below as he got faster and faster. He was gaining on the Christmasaurus, who was now just up ahead, his tail swishing temptingly behind him, almost close enough for Marvin to reach.

Only two more pushes and . . .

'GOT YOU!'

Marvin cried, as he grabbed hold of the escaping dinosaur's tail.

What he didn't realize was that this was exactly what the Christmasaurus had planned!

Quickly, the Christmasaurus bounced up from the pavement and into the air, pulling Marvin up with him into what had to be the world record for the highest ollie.

Marvin reached down, holding on to the skateboard with one hand while gripping the flying dinosaur's tail with the other, as together they soared up and away.

'WHOA! This is awesome!'

Marvin cheered, looking down at the world far below the wheels of his flying skateboard!

The Christmasaurus grinned and swooped down low over the houses, pulling Marvin along as he skated across the rooftops, grinded the gutters and ollied the chimneys.

'**Yahoo!**' Marvin screamed with pure joy as they landed in the middle of a wide-open field.

'OK, *that* was the coolest thing ever! Wait until my brother hears about this. Oh man, I wish he was here to see it! I can't wait to tell him. . .' Marvin trailed off and a flash of sadness crossed his face. '*If* he's still talking to me.'

'Oi! Who are you?' someone yelled, running towards them across the field. 'This is a private training pitch. You're not meant to be here!'

'No . . . WAY!' Marvin's jaw dropped.

'That's Harry Walker!'

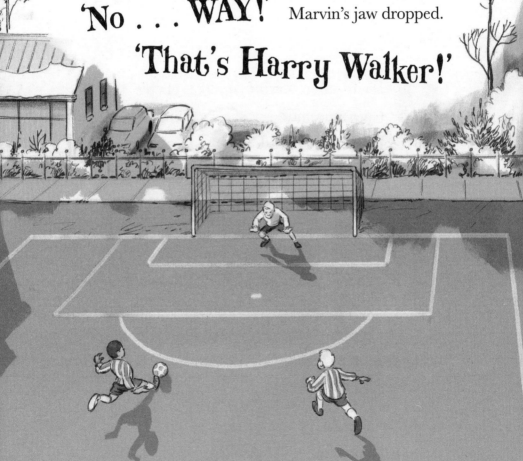

CHAPTER TWENTY

FOOTBALL-O-SAURUS

Marvin stood in the middle of his favourite team's training pitch, gawping at his all-time favourite player running towards him and the blue dinosaur who had just flown him across town. This was turning into a very odd day.

'I don't believe it. You're Harry Walker! You're the best player of all time!' Marvin spluttered excitedly.

'Thanks, mate! But listen: I don't know how you got in here, but we don't allow fans into the training sessions, and especially not with pets. What even is that thing?' Walker asked.

'Oh . . . this? Erm . . . this is . . .' Marvin didn't know what to say – he'd only just met the Christmasaurus and didn't know a thing about this strange dinosaur who had just appeared in his life!

But the Christmasaurus had a plan. He started jumping up and down, waving his arms around like some sort of strange dance routine, before pointing up to the enormous posters around the training ground, all showing a huge advert:

MASCOT TRY-OUTS TODAY!

'Oh, so your friend wants to be our new mascot. Nice touch bringing your own suit!' Harry Walker chuckled. 'That's the best dinosaur costume I've ever seen! Can I try it on?'

He started to walk towards the Christmasaurus with his hands out, ready to try to take his head off when –

'On yer 'ead, Walker!'

A football was tearing through the air towards them!

Harry Walker started to turn, but the ball was going too fast and seemed to be aiming straight for Marvin's head. He closed his eyes and waited for the

WHACK!

Except . . . the whack never came, because the
Christmasaurus had leapt across the pitch, putting
himself between the ball and Marvin. If Marvin had
opened his eyes, he would have seen a scene worthy
of a slow-motion action replay on *Match of the Day* as
the Christmasaurus launched into the air and volleyed
the football with his right claw, just like Harry Walker's
winning goal last season, sending it to the back of the
net.

'WHAT A GOAL!'

Harry Walker cheered as the Christmasaurus slid across the grass in celebration.

'That was an incredible shot! Are you sure you want to be a mascot?' Harry Walker asked the Christmasaurus with admiration. 'You could be a player with reactions like that!'

'Really?' Marvin said, opening his eyes and sounding disappointed. 'I didn't see it!'

'Hey, do you want some advice? Next time a ball is flying towards your face, don't close your eyes!' Harry Walker said. Marvin nodded, hanging on to his football hero's every word. 'Always keep your eye on the ball and look around. OK? Keep practising and you might even be wearing one of these shirts one day! In fact . . .' Walker slipped off his Trumpton City training shirt and handed it to Marvin. (Don't worry – he had a long-sleeved top underneath so he wasn't too cold!)

'No way,' Marvin whispered in total shock.

'Yes way! Now, get your friend to the mascot try-outs! Good luck!' Harry Walker called to the Christmasaurus, giving him a thumbs up as he ran back to his team-mates at the other end of the pitch.

'This is seriously the **BEST** day ever. Braydon is not going to believe I met the actual Harry Walker! I can't wait to show him this top. We watch him play all the time! Never miss a game . . . Well, at least, I never used to,' Marvin said, suddenly realizing he'd missed quite a few real matches while playing football games on the GameBox instead. He shook away the thought as he slipped on the red-and-white shirt.

'I can't believe you scored that goal. I would definitely have missed that shot. I haven't kicked a football since –' Marvin stopped The Christmasaurus knew what he was about to say. 'Since I got the GameBox.'

As he looked at the sleek console that was still clutched in the Christmasaurus's claws, Marvin noticed how much better real life felt.

'Wow, I hadn't realized how much I've missed playing football. No matter how high-definition that screen is, it can never beat the feeling of your foot connecting with a ball, or the vibration of a skateboard rolling over concrete, or playing ping-pong with –'

Right then, at that very moment, it felt to Marvin as though everything had been blurry and was suddenly coming into focus as he remembered what he loved doing more than anything in the whole wide world.

He thought back over the past year: to the holidays, the family trips, the birthday parties, the celebrations . . . all his memories were blocked by a big GameBox screen right smack in the centre. But, in the background, there was always someone by his side – one person he'd been ignoring for too long.

'– Braydon,' he whispered.

He gasped as it dawned on him exactly where he was meant to be right now. He looked at the enormous digital clock hanging at the end of the football pitch that said 1.45 p.m.

He heard his brother's voice in his mind: '*Registration to enter the doubles tournament closes at two o'clock. I'll be there.*

THE CHRISTMASAURUS AND THE NAUGHTY LIST

Two brothers, one team . . .'

'Hey, I don't suppose you could give me a ride somewhere, could you?' Marvin asked his dino companion, picking up his skateboard.

The Christmasaurus let out a little excited roar and held out his tail, ready to fly. The moment he felt Marvin grab hold, he launched across the Trumpton City training pitch, pulling Marvin behind him as his skateboard carved a long trail across the perfect grass.

As they accelerated towards the fast-approaching goalposts, the Christmasaurus took off, and Marvin popped the highest ollie he could, grabbing the skateboard with his fingertips as they raced into the air once more.

CHAPTER TWENTY-ONE

PING GETS HIS PONG BACK

Braydon paced back and forth around the foyer of the enormous event hall where the Junior Ping-Pong Championship was being held. To his left was the registration desk for the singles tournament. On his right, the registration desk for the doubles tournament. On the wall directly in front of him was a clock telling him that there was only one minute and twenty-two seconds left until registration closed.

He was going to have to sign in for singles.

Braydon let out a deep sigh and shook his head, annoyed that he'd even allowed himself to hope that his brother might actually turn up.

The old Marvin would have been here, if his mind hadn't been taken over by GamerDork500! Braydon thought, as he dragged his feet to the singles registration table.

'Two brothers . . .' a voice called from behind him.

Braydon spun on the spot to see Marvin standing in the entrance.

'One team . . .' Braydon replied.

'ONE DREAM!'

they cheered together for the first time since Marvin had been given the GameBox.

'You came!' Braydon said with a huge smile.

'Well, a promise is a promise, lil' bro. There's a trophy here with our name on it.' Marvin grinned.

'What made you ditch the GameBox?'

Marvin stole a secret glance up to the skylight above the foyer, where the Christmasaurus was looking down and waving excitedly.

'I guess I just forgot to look up.'

'Well, to be honest, GamerKidd3000 has been a RUBBISH big brother.'

PING GETS HIS PONG BACK

Marvin already knew it, but it was still hard to hear Braydon say it out loud. Ditching football games or cinema trips for a video game was one thing, but ditching his little brother? Marvin didn't even need to see his name on the Naughty List to know how wrong that was. He'd never felt so disappointed in himself.

'You're right.' Marvin sighed. 'GamerKidd3000 was a rubbish big bro.'

'But . . .' Braydon smiled and reached inside his backpack. 'I knew *Marvin* would never let me down. I even packed your paddle!'

'Thanks. I've got something for you too,' Marvin said as he took off the Trumpton City training shirt and handed it to his brother.

'No way! Where did you get this?'

'It's a long story and we've only got thirty seconds left to register, so I'll tell you later!' he said as they ran as fast as they could to the registration desk.

'You're just in time,' said the old, moustached man behind the registration desk, smiling. 'Team name?'

Marvin and Braydon looked at each other and nodded.

'THE PONGERS!'

The man raised his eyebrows and signed them in. 'OK then, Pongers, let's hope you don't stink! Your first match starts in five minutes on Table Two. You're up against Double Vision. Tournament rules – first team to eleven points wins.'

The brothers entered the auditorium, where hundreds of seated people were watching the players warm up. Ahead of them, in the centre of the room, were four ping-pong tables bathed in white spotlights and surrounded by the players they'd be facing throughout the day.

'There's Table Two,' said Marvin, pointing. A boy and girl around their age were stretching and squatting next to the table, clearly preparing themselves for the match.

'Hey, we're the Pongers. Are you Double Vision?' Braydon asked.

'Sorry, we don't talk to *enemies*,' snarked the girl as she balanced a spinning a ping-pong paddle on her index finger.

The awkward moment was interrupted by the lights dimming and an epic trumpet fanfare blasting out of nowhere.

'Ladies and gentlemen,' a commentator boomed over the PA system. 'Please give it up for the reigning Junior Ping-Pong Championship champions, the Paddle Bros!'

Percy and Paul Paddle came knee-sliding into the auditorium to wild cheers from the crowd.

'Thank you! Thank you!' Percy Paddle said while peering over his mirrored sunglasses at their screaming fans in the crowd.

'That's lame,' Braydon whispered to Marvin.

'*So* lame,' confirmed Marvin. 'Promise me we'll never be them!'

'Yeah, let's just *beat* them!' And, with that, they high-fived with their paddles.

'First we have to beat Double *Losers*,' said Marvin.

'We heard that!' whined Double Vision in unison.

'Oh, I thought you didn't talk to enemies!' Braydon smiled as the referee blew the whistle and the first games began.

While all this had been going on below, the Christmasaurus had been leaping across the roof, peering through the skylights that looked down on the championship. As he watched the games get started, he couldn't help but duck and weave with each shot that was fired at Marvin and Braydon. They narrowly avoided defeat a few times while Marvin got back into the swing of playing a game in real life, having to use his whole body and not just his fingers!

They worked as a team, Braydon covering for Marvin while his muscles warmed up and he remembered the feel of the paddle as it sliced through the air, the soft ping of the ball connecting with the table and the trust he had in his team-mate.

By the final round of the first game, he was returning shots with seemingly superhuman reflexes. The Christmasaurus could barely keep up with the white blur of the ball as it pinged this way and ponged that way, back and forth across the table at impossible speed.

Each time Marvin and Braydon scored, he did a little spin and roared into the air in celebration, occasionally loud enough for Marvin to hear and look up at him with a big winning grin on his face.

It wasn't long before the first match was over. Marvin and Braydon had totally wiped the floor with Double Vision, and next up they were faced with the Serve Sisters.

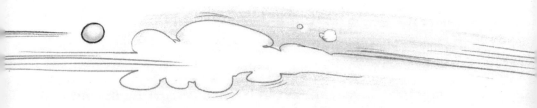

The Christmasaurus watched the rival team serve spectacular spins that made the ball turn in totally unpredictable directions, but the Pongers were all over it:

DUCKING and
WEAVING,
SLICING and DIVING,

returning every single shot until they had sent the Serve Sisters out of the championship!

The Christmasaurus flew a lap round the roof in his excitement (luckily the crowds were so absorbed by the fierce matches in front of them that they didn't notice a blue dinosaur hovering above their heads!). The Pongers had made it to the semi-final, and things were getting tense now as they faced the Unreachables – the tallest players in the Junior Championship.

These two were as tall as Marvin and Braydon standing on each other's shoulders! Their arms were so long they looked like over-stretched Stretch Armstrong dolls that would never shrink back to their original size – and these super-long arms could reach the ball wherever their opponent sent it, making them a formidable foe to face.

The Christmasaurus suddenly spotted Marvin whispering something into Braydon's ear.

Did the brothers have a game plan?

PING GETS HIS PONG BACK

The Unreachables served first – PING!

Braydon sent the ball shooting across the net –

PONG!

It came back the moment it had bounced – PING!

Marvin fired it back to the opposite side of the table –

PONG!

An Unreachable player stretched his arm across the table to return it – PING!

Braydon spun it far across to the opposite side of the table –

PONG!

Meaning that an Unreachable had to stretch his long, bendy arm out for it again – **P I N G !**

PONG!

PING!

PONG!

PING GETS HIS PONG BACK

Marvin and Braydon switched the direction of the ball with every shot, forcing their opponents to stretch and reach and twist their flailing arms all over the place to keep up, until . . .

'**Ow!**' the Unreachables yelped. Their arms had somehow wrapped around each other's and become stuck! Marvin and Braydon's unpredictable shots had made them flap their bendy arms about so wildly that they had unknowingly become tangled up together in some sort of strange bendy-arm-knot!

The Unreachables fell to the floor, trying to pull themselves free, but the harder they pulled, the tighter their arms became locked together! They had no choice but to forfeit the game.

Marvin and Braydon were through to the FINAL!

This was it.

They were about to come face to face with their biggest rivals, their ping-pong arch-nemeses: the Paddle Bros.

'So, we meet again, Pongers.' Paul Paddle smirked.

'It's *THE* Pongers,' corrected Braydon.

'It doesn't matter what your name is, my brother has seen the future and – SPOILER ALERT – you don't win!' Percy Paddle said, and the brothers cracked up laughing.

Braydon was about to say something back but Marvin put his hand out to stop him.

'Let your paddle do the talking,' he told his brother as their opponents mimed ringing an imaginary doorbell on the opposite side of the table.

'DING-DONG!
Let's play PING-PONG!'

they chanted together before launching the first serve over the net, and so the game was on.

It was a rocky start for Marvin and Braydon. The Christmasaurus could barely watch as they were pushed to the limit of their ping-pong abilities.

The crowd cheered and gasped as the match got closer and closer. The Paddle Bros gained a one-point lead, then Marvin and Braydon pulled it back . . . then lost it again . . . then won it back again. It was SO close!

Suddenly Paul Paddle's backhand drive clipped the edge of the table, sending the ball shooting to the side of the court. Sure that they had won the point, the Paddle Bros punched the air in celebration, but Braydon leapt for the stray ball that was still in play! His outstretched paddle connected with it and returned the shot while Paul and Percy were busy high-fiving.

The crowd went WILD!

The score was now TEN–NINE to the Pongers. Just one more point and the trophy was theirs!

Braydon threw the ball up and served a whizzing shot across the table, but the Paddle Bros returned it easily.

PING!

PONG!

PING!

PONG!

Neither of the sets of brothers were going to let a point drop – the trophy was at stake!

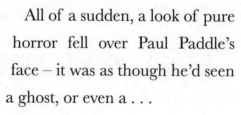

All of a sudden, a look of pure horror fell over Paul Paddle's face – it was as though he'd seen a ghost, or even a . . .

'DINOSAUR!'

he screamed, pointing to the
skylight over the championship, having
spotted the Christmasaurus on the roof just as Percy
sent a backhand drive pinging over the net.

Time seemed to slow down as the whole auditorium
turned to look in the direction that Paul was pointing,
even Braydon. However, Marvin, who was already well
aware of the dinosaur on the roof, thought of the advice
Harry Walker had given him earlier: '*Next time a ball is
flying towards your face, don't close your eyes!*'

So Marvin did just that. With his eyes locked on the
zooming ball, he pulled back his paddle and released
an almighty return that spun over the net in one
direction, then bounced in a completely different one.
The '**ping**' of the ball on the table brought the Paddle
Bros' attention back to the game, but it was TOO
LATE! They dived straight into each other's arms and
collapsed in a defeated heap on the floor!

'AND THE PONGERS WIN THE CHAMPIONSHIP!'

blasted the commentator, as the crowd went wild.

The Christmasaurus watched with proud tears in his eyes as Marvin and Braydon were presented with the trophy and their parents came running out of the crowd to congratulate them.

'Two brothers . . .' said Marvin, beaming.

'One team . . .' added Braydon.

'ONE DREAM!'

they both cheered, lifting the trophy into the air.

❄

That evening in Marvin's bedroom, the brothers sat on the bed, staring at their reflection in the golden trophy.

'Do you think Mum will let us eat our cereal out of it?' Braydon asked.

'No way!' Marvin replied, and Braydon smiled.

'I can't believe the Paddle Bros tried to fake seeing a dinosaur during the game,' he said. 'I mean, if you're going to play the whole "What's that behind you?" trick, then at least make it believable.' Braydon laughed as he used his sleeve to polish out a fingerprint on the trophy's shiny surface, but his face suddenly paled as he spotted something in the reflection.

He whipped round and ran to the window.

'What's wrong?' Marvin asked.

'I thought I saw a . . .' Braydon shook his head.

'A what?'

'I must be giddy from winning the trophy. For a moment *I* thought I saw a dinosaur!' Braydon chuckled.

'That *is* weird,' said Marvin, smiling as he joined his brother at the window.

'Hey, isn't that your GameBox out there?' Braydon asked, pointing to his brother's prized possession on the rooftop as snowflakes started to settle on the 4K3D super-megapixel screen.

'Oh, yeah,' said Marvin casually, closing the curtains and leaving it out there. 'We can rescue it tomorrow . . . So, do you want to know how I got that Harry Walker shirt?'

Braydon grinned. **'YES!'**

PING GETS HIS PONG BACK

As Marvin began telling his brother all about the adventures of the day, the Christmasaurus was vanishing into the night with a slightly lighter Naughty List in his claws.

CHAPTER TWENTY-TWO

ELLA NOYING

Ella Noying hated vegetables. Carrots? Gross! Broccoli? Total barf-fest. And it was really best not to mention . . . Well, she can't even bear to hear *THIS* vegetable said out loud, so it's probably best if I just write the words very small and you read them in your head:

BRUSSELS SPROUTS!

To Ella, BRUSSELS SPROUTS were the worst thing ever invented in the history of everything gross, and whoever thought it was a good idea for them to be a part of her country's traditional Christmas dinner must have totally hated Christmas. That was the only explanation.

Cook them for too long and sprouts were like green balls of smushy, grassy mud! But they were even worse when they were undercooked and crunchy – like eating a tree's eyeball!

Ella hadn't always hated vegetables, though. There had been a time when she'd quite liked a nice runner bean or two, or even the occasional floret of roasted cauliflower, but over the last year that had changed. And it was all because of the stinky, enormous waste-recycling centre –

aka great big dump!

– that was on the outskirts of Ella's hometown of Whiffington.

The rubbish dump had always been there, but recently the people of Whiffington had been using it a lot more to get rid of their unwanted things. You see, the dump contained a special bit of

DARK,
spooky magic

that eventually made everything the humans of the town didn't want disappear! (But that's a story for another book – which I *highly* recommend you read . . .) Unfortunately, the stink didn't seem to vanish quite as quickly as the rubbish!

All you really need to know to understand how Whiffington Dump had made Ella suddenly **HATE** vegetables is that it was right behind her house, and for a year steamy, veggie pongs had been wafting on the breeze through Ella's bedroom window.

YUCK!

Now, whenever Ella was faced with a pile of green veg on her dinner plate, all she thought of was the stinky dump and everyone's rotten waste. Which was why she'd been doing her very best to dodge every splodge of the green stuff.

For example, she used to love avocado on toast for her breakfast (yes, Smarty Pants, I know avocado is actually a fruit, but it's green, so it still counts!), but now Ella only ate Sugar-Flakes. At lunch, she always walked speedily past the trays of vegetables in the school cafeteria, trying not to make eye contact with the dinner lady as she piled chips (we meet again, Smarty Pants! Yes, chips are made of potato, which is a vegetable, but we all know that doesn't count either!) and slices of pizza on to her plate.

'You're supposed to have a portion of vegetables with your school lunch,' said one of her best friends, Norman Quirk, to her one day.

'Says who?' Ella replied confidently.

'The big sign on the wall,' said Ella's other BFF, Lucy Dungston.

Ella didn't need to look at the sign because she knew full well that she was breaking the rules, but when she looked at Norman and Lucy's plates and saw green pepper stuffed with more green pepper and topped with oily brown mushrooms, it made her want to **puke**! So, she just grinned like she didn't care and took a bite of the hot cheesy pizza.

Avoiding vegetables at school was one thing, but dodging them at home was a top-secret operation. It took brains. It took courage. It took secretly stuffing your pockets full of mushy peas.

Why?

Because Ella's mum was a . . . (drum roll) . . .

VEGETARIAN!
DUN DUN DUUUUUUN!

That's right – Mrs Noying loved nothing more than cabbage mush and pea slosh, or broccoli gloop and asparagus twigs. It was like Ella's mum's tastebuds were programmed to be the exact opposite of her daughter's.

And it gets worse.

Not only was Mrs Noying a vegetarian, she was also **THE WORST COOK ON THE PLANET!** Or at least the worst cook in Whiffington. Which was why, luckily for Ella, it was usually Mr Noying who did all the cooking. But that all changed when Mrs Noying rescued a dusty old vegetarian cookbook from . . . you guessed it . . . **THE DUMP!**

'Mum, there was a reason someone threw that thing away!' Ella complained when her mum arrived home with the damp book in her hands. 'It looks pretty disgusting.'

217

'No, Ella, it's a sign!' Mrs Noying said excitedly. 'I used to love cooking, and always dreamt of being a chef when I was your age. Then just the other day I was thinking about digging out the slow cooker –'

'Why do you want to cook things slowly?' Ella interrupted. 'You know there's *FAST FOOD* now, right?'

'I'm serious, Ella. I was thinking about cooking again and then what do I find sticking out of the dump?'

'A cookbook,' Ella replied with a sigh.

'Not just any cookbook. A *vegetarian* cookbook!' Mrs Noying cheered, waving *Around the World in Eighty Vegetables*. 'You know, I used to cook all the time with my mum when I was your age. We can work our way through the book together, mother and daughter.' She beamed at Ella.

'I don't want to be a chef, Mum. I want to be an explorer! Sail the world, trek in the mountains, stand at the North Pole!'

'Well, even explorers need to eat!' Her mum grinned, not giving up without a fight and leaving Ella no choice but to use the most classic excuse of all time, an excuse that no parent can argue with . . .

'I have homework to do!' Ella lied.

'OK, well, I suppose that should come first. I'll call you when dinner's ready!' Mrs Noying squeaked with excitement as she began pulling pots and pans out of the cupboards.

About an hour later, Ella caught a sniff of something truly gross.

'Ew, that disgusting dump STINKS!' she muttered to herself as she went to close her window – only to make the horrifying discovery that her window was already CLOSED.

The pong was coming from downstairs . . .

From INSIDE her house!

And Ella had the tummy-churning feeling that it was coming from the kitchen. It was like wet, slimy . . . mud! That's the only way she could describe the smell. Mud. Thick, sloppy mud.

'Ella! Dinner!' came Mrs Noying's sing-song voice up to her daughter.

Reluctantly, Ella dragged herself down the stairs

where, slung over the bottom of the banister, was her green hoodie, the one with the big pocket on the front.

DING!

It gave Ella an idea, and she slipped the hoodie over her head as she sat down at the dining table opposite her dad, who had a terrified expression on his face as he stared at his plate. It was piled high with a mountain of steaming green mulch that looked like it belonged in a wheelbarrow.

'How is it, darling?' Mrs Noying asked her husband as she placed Ella's plate in front of her.

'It's . . . thick,' Mr Noying mumbled through a mouthful of stewed leaves that he was trying to pluck up the courage to swallow.

'Yes?'

'And . . . slimy?' Mr Noying spluttered. Then he saw the look of sadness spreading over his wife's face at the thought of her food not tasting very nice. 'But delicious!' he lied, gulping the mouthful down with a sweaty smile.

'Really?' Mrs Noying said hopefully.

'Oh, yes, once you get used to the lumps,' he replied with a grin.

'And what do you think, Ella?' Mrs Noying asked, turning round only to find that her daughter's plate was already totally clear.

'Oh, it was scrummy!' Ella said, leaning back in her chair and rubbing her tummy. 'I mean, I wasn't sure at first, you know, what with the way it smells . . .'

'And looks!' added Mr Noying.

'Yes. But that was yummy, Mum!' Ella said.

'Well, let me get you some more!' Mrs Noying sprang to her feet, ready to reload Ella's plate.

'**NO!**' Ella screamed, stopping her mum before she could serve her any more slop. 'I mean . . . I'm just so full already. I couldn't eat another bite. Can I go and finish my homework?'

'Of course, darling. You can have the leftovers for lunch tomorrow,' said Mrs Noying with a smile.

The moment she got to her bedroom, Ella stuck her hands into the big pocket on the front of her hoodie and pulled out a pile of gloppy green goo. That's right

– in case you hadn't already guessed, Ella hadn't eaten the horrible slop but had instead shoved it ALL in her pocket. The problem was that now she needed to find a hiding place where her mum wouldn't find it. Not because she didn't want to get into trouble, but her mum had been so proud of her cooking that Ella didn't want to hurt her feelings!

In a matter of seconds, the sloppy veg had ponged up Ella's bedroom, and she quickly ran to the window to let some fresh air in. Only there wasn't any fresh air outside! Instead she was hit in the face by a breeze, carrying with it the pongy whiff from . . .

'The dump!' Ella whispered with a mischievous grin, suddenly knowing exactly where she was going to put her mum's disgusting dinner. Those veggies were going back to where they belonged . . .

CHAPTER TWENTY-THREE

DUMPING DINNER

That night, Ella waited for her mum and dad to kiss her goodnight, keeping one eye on the bulging, squelchy pocket of the hoodie she'd worn to dinner and hoping her mum wouldn't spot it.

The moment she heard her parents turn out the light, she slid out of bed, slipped into the now slightly slimy hoodie and did the thing that is the reason she's on the Naughty List . . .

Now, before you read this next part, I have to warn you: DO NOT TRY THIS AT HOME. Seriously, don't even think about it or both of us will get in big trouble. OK?

Ella secretly
SNEAKED OUT OF HER HOUSE!

Sneaking out of her house wasn't just a bad idea – it was a

REALLY,

SUPER-DUPER,

DANGEROUS,

TERRIBLE idea.

First, Ella had to climb out of her bedroom window, then slide down the slippery drainpipe until her feet felt the soft mud of the flower bed. But that was only the beginning of her treacherous quest to vanish the veg.

Next, she had to crawl through the flower bed so she didn't trigger the security light and wake up all the neighbours.

Then it was climbing through a loose panel in the wooden fence into next-door's garden, without

disturbing the Ratcliffes' dog, Prowler, who liked to sleep with his drooling head poking out of the cat flap.

Once past the snoozing guard dog of drool, it was up and over the wire fence and into the *Alley of Shadows*. I mean, obviously that wasn't its real name. It was basically a little path that ran along the back of all the gardens on their street, but she couldn't access it from her house without trampling on her mother's attempt at a vegetable patch, which had so far only managed to produce a rather small (and green!) tomato. At that time of night, when the grown-ups were asleep, the alley was dark. No, it was *darker* than dark. It was as black as a starless universe, and Ella felt a chill run down her spine as she looked into its depths.

What am I doing? she thought, slipping her hands into her damp hoodie pocket to feel the sludgy substance. Surely this was far enough to get rid of the evidence?

She was about to tip the lot on to the grassy verge at the side of the dark alley, but then suddenly remembered that this was on her mum's daily running route! What if she stepped in it the next day? We've all stepped in dog poop before, but veggie slop? Her mum would know it was her own cooking instantly, and Ella would be done for! Not just for hiding the dinner, but for sneaking out at night!

No, this wasn't far enough yet. She needed to get to the dump; it was the only way to dispose of the evidence entirely!

So Ella took a breath (she wasn't sure why but it seemed to help keep the scary stuff away) and walked into the Alley of Shadows.

The darkness fell on her like a heavy blanket, and suddenly Ella couldn't tell which way was forward or which way was back. All she could do was keep walking and follow her nose towards the wafting whiff of her destination.

A few stinky steps later, Ella stepped into a pool of green light cast by the unmistakable Creaker-friendly street lights on the recently named Woleb Avenue. (Creakers are, of course, the creatures that live under your bed and make all those noises you hear in your house at night. There aren't any in this story, but there is *another book* all about them. Just saying.)

Almost there . . .
almost there . . .

Ella thought, as she climbed the wire gate at the entrance to the dump. She quickly found the container that said **GREEN WASTE** and emptied the contents of her hoodie pocket into it before slinking quietly back the way she'd come – through the green lights, into the blackness of the Alley of Shadows, past Prowler (still drooling out of the cat flap), across the Ratcliffes' garden, through the loose fence panel, along the flower bed, up the drainpipe and finally in through her bedroom window.

She collapsed on to her bed, her heart pounding in her chest from the naughty excitement. Ella hated to admit it, but, as a smile crept over her face, she realized that she had kind of enjoyed her secret adventure in the dark.

'*Bon appetit!*' Mrs Noying beamed as she served dinner the next evening.

'What is that?' Mr Noying coughed as the steam shot up his nostrils.

'Funghi-stuffed funghi.'

'It doesn't look very fun to me,' joked Mr Noying, but Ella knew her mum had put a lot of time and effort into this revolting dish, so she ignored her dad and tried her best to look impressed at the plate of food that smelt like the dump.

'So, it's a mushroom stuffed with mashed-up mushrooms?' asked Mr Noying as he scooped up a little of the soggy brown mush with his fork.

'Exactly! What do you think?'

Mr Noying brought the fork of funghi closer to his mouth. It looked more like a live slug, and it wobbled like a lump of brown jelly as he slurped it up.

'Well?' Mrs Noying asked hopefully.

'Ummm . . . .

it's quite . . .

SLIMY . . . isn't it?'

'Yes, I think it's meant to be a little slimy,' Mrs Noying said with a nod.

'And quite . . .
CHEWY?'

'Right,' Mrs Noying noted, but a sad expression fell over her face as she started to realize that perhaps her cooking might not be quite as yummy as she'd hoped.

'But, I mean, really it's quite . . . *edible*. Isn't it, Dad?' Ella beamed, and to Mr Noying's surprise – and Mrs Noying's delight – Ella's plate of sloppy mushrooms stuffed with more sloppy mushrooms was totally clean.

Ella gave an angelic smile. 'All finished!'

'Already?' Mr Noying gawped.

'Oh, yes! Thank you, Mum. May I leave the table?'

'Of course you can, my hungry little one. That's the second meal you've eaten from my veggie cookbook. I knew it was a good find!'

And, with that, Ella waddled out of the dining room with pockets stuffed with mushrooms stuffed with mushrooms!

A few hours later, once her parents had wished her goodnight, Ella was off again on her quest to the dump to ditch her stash of disgusting dinner, and it wasn't long before this secret, dangerous, naughty escapade became her nightly routine. Soon her dark journey was made lighter by the fairy lights in the windows, but, with Christmas approaching, Ella knew it wouldn't just bring stockings by the fire and holly wreaths on the doors. It would also bring with it vegetables that already smelt like Whiffington Dump even before her mum got her hands on them: BRUSSELS SPROUTS.

What she didn't know was that it would also be bringing a dinosaur on the roof.

CHAPTER TWENTY-FOUR

SPROUTS

'**B**russels sprouts!' Mrs Noying cheered as she burst into the living room with a pan overflowing with green clouds of steam.

'Oh . . . goody.' Mr Noying gulped.

'Now, I know you've never been a fan of sprouts in the past, Ella, but, given you've loved my cooking so much, I really think this new poached sprout recipe from my book might just convert you!' Mrs Noying smiled hopefully as she served a heaped ladle of green balls on to Ella's plate.

'Blimey, that's a lot of Brussels!' Mr Noying chuckled

at the sprout mountain on his daughter's plate.

'Don't worry, there's plenty for you too, dear,' trilled Mrs Noying as she dolloped twice as many on to her husband's plate.

Ella had to pinch her own leg to stop herself laughing as she watched her poor dad force a fork into a rock-hard sprout. **PING!**

The ball of green shot across the room,

CRASHING

into the clock on the wall.

'Are they meant to be this hard?' Mr Noying asked his wife, trying to sound polite.

'Oh, yes, chefs call it *al dente*,' Mrs Noying informed him.

'We'll need an *al dentist* after biting these!' he whispered to Ella, only to find that her plate was already empty.

'Well, well, well, someone seems to have lost her doubts about sprouts!' Mrs Noying beamed, and Ella felt a little fizz of joy inside at seeing how happy her empty plate had made her mum.

'Oh, yes, they were delicious! Can I go and do my homework now?' Ella asked.

'Of course. Run along!'

Ella lifted up her school bag, which she had started keeping under the dinner table at mealtimes.

'That looks heavy tonight. What have you got in there?' Mr Noying asked suspiciously. He had a hard sprout stuffed in his cheek, making him look like a hamster.

'Oh, you know, just . . . books and stuff,' Ella said, but if Mr Noying had had X-ray vision he wouldn't have seen books in Ella's bag. He would have seen something more like this . . .

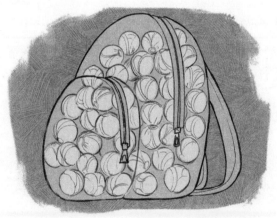

SPROUTS

That's right! Ella's school bag was absolutely crammed full of sprouts! It was her new veg-transporter. She'd realized early on that if veg-dumping was going to be a regular event, then using her hoodie pocket was not efficient enough, and there was always a risk that a rogue sprout or two might roll out. Her school bag could fit ten times more vegetables inside it, and there was zero chance of hurting her mum's feelings (plus it made descending the drainpipe and dodging drooling dogs a lot easier). In fact, the more Ella ran this nightly veg-avoidance gauntlet, the more she began to enjoy it, and she found herself ducking and weaving with a smile upon her face.

The journey had become automatic now. *Drainpipe, flower bed, security light* – she hardly needed to think about what she was doing – *hole in the fence, drooling dog, over the gate* – she'd never eat vegetables again – *Alley of Shadows, dinosaur, green light* –

Ella froze with one foot still dipped in the pool of green light. Did she just see what she thought she saw?

Surely not. IMPOSSIBLE!

But something was keeping her frozen with fear. Deep down, she knew that those two prehistoric eyeballs that she'd seen glaring at her weren't in her imagination, and there was, in fact, a dinosaur crouching in the shadows.

'P-p-please don't eat me!' Ella slowly turned to face the fearsome blue beast as it slowly leant in towards her, opened its cold jaws and . . . licked her across the face with its big sloppy tongue!

'Ew! That's *so* gross!' Ella said, wiping away the dino-drool as the Christmasaurus chuckled to himself.

'Are you laughing?' she asked, feeling less scared and more embarrassed now.

The Christmasaurus nodded.

'I didn't know dinosaurs laughed. Wait . . . I didn't know dinosaurs *existed*. Am I dreaming?'

Ella stared at the frosted scales that covered the Christmasaurus as they glistened in the green street light. The dinosaur took a step forward and bent his head down low, like a dog asking to be stroked. Ella was so curious that she didn't hesitate to place her hands on to his cool skin.

'Wow, you *are* real,' Ella whispered. 'What is a dinosaur doing walking the streets of Whiffington in the middle of the night?'

The Christmasaurus stepped back into the shadows and returned a moment later with a thick black book between his teeth. He dropped it on to the pavement in the middle of the glow from the street light and let Ella read the words on the front.

'Naughty List? Whoa, as in *the* Naughty List? Santa's actual "checking it twice" Naughty List? You know Santa?' Ella said, as though she were standing in the presence of an A-list celebrity.

The Christmasaurus nodded.

'OMG! Wait until I tell Lucy and Norman. They will not believe . . . hold it. Why are you showing me this?' Ella said.

He let out a frustrated huff through his nostrils and nudged her school bag with his nose.

'What's in my bag is none of your business,' Ella snapped.

The Christmasaurus spun round and flicked the Naughty List open with a swish of his tail. The pages flapped back and forth with a mind of their own, before abruptly stopping on a page with a name glowing with a brilliant golden shimmer.

ELLA NOYING

Ella stared at her name for a minute or two. It was never easy for a child to realize they were on the Naughty List, let alone when a dinosaur drops the news at their feet in the middle of the night *and* while they're halfway through doing the thing that got them on the Naughty List in the first place.

'Is it for lying to my parents?' Ella asked.

The Christmasaurus snorted a definite no.

'For not eating my greens?'

Another growled NO from Ella's new dinosaur companion, for the Christmasaurus knew exactly why Ella was on the Naughty List. He recognized her from the flickering shadows cast by the green candle on the ceiling of Santa's reading room.

In the distance, the bell from Whiffington's church chimed midnight, and a cold breeze rattled past them, giving Ella a chill.

'I should be getting home,' she said with a shiver, pulling her jacket a little tighter.

As she said the word 'home', the letters of her name pulsed even brighter, before fading slightly to settle a little dimmer than they were before.

'Oh,' said Ella, understanding now. 'I'm on the Naughty List for sneaking out of my house, aren't I?'

The Christmasaurus nodded and closed the list.

'I know it's wrong, but I just can't eat my mum's cooking. It's beyond gross. If I put it in my mouth, I think I might actually puke at the dinner table, and that would hurt Mum's feelings, wouldn't it? So there's no way I'm doing that, but I can't throw it in the bin at home either because then she'd know I'm not eating it, and that would hurt her feelings too! So really I'm doing something nice!' Ella said, trying to defend her actions. 'Try it for yourself if you don't believe me.'

She took off her backpack, unzipped it and plonked it

on the floor under the Christmasaurus's nose.

He peered into it and saw the green sprouts all squished inside.

His tail started wagging excitedly – he was starving! Of course, he would have preferred a big bag of candy canes, or cinnamon cookies, or anything other than vegetables. BUT, of all the veggies, at least these were Christmassy ones. He plunged his snout inside the bag and took a big mouthful . . . then spat the whole lot back out, spraying Ella with a gallon of

sprout slush.

SPROUTS

Not only did the sprouts hurt his wobbly tooth, but the taste was so bad it actually *hurt his tongue*!

'See what I mean?' said Ella, laughing.

The Christmasaurus let out a sigh and looked her in the eyes.

'I know. You're right. It doesn't matter how bad they taste, or if I'm trying not to hurt Mum's feelings – it's still wrong to sneak out of the house.'

The Christmasaurus grunted.

'Yes, and dangerous.'

He huffed.

'OK, I promise I won't do it again!' Ella mumbled unconvincingly, causing the Christmasaurus to growl.

'I just can't eat these revolting things my mum insists on cooking! Bland veg, veg, veg, every single day. Why can't there be a way to make vegetables taste good?'

The Christmasaurus suddenly started jumping around like an excited puppy.

'What is it?' Ella asked as the Christmasaurus scooped up her backpack with one of his icy spines and crouched down low next to her, ready for her to climb aboard.

'Are we going somewhere?' Ella asked, hopping on to his back.

The Christmasaurus nodded excitedly. He knew exactly who could help with this veg-mergency!

CHAPTER TWENTY-FIVE

ELLA AND THE ELVES

Ella squeezed her arms around the Christmasaurus's neck as he galloped through pools of green light, straight towards the entrance of Whiffington Dump.

'Slow down! The gates are locked!' Ella cried at seeing the metal wire rapidly getting

closer, closer, CLOSER!

But the Christmasaurus didn't slow down. He ran

faster, faster, FASTER!

'We're going to crash!' Ella yelled, but, just as they should have smashed into the gates, the Christmasaurus leapt into the air, whooshing up and over the entrance to the dump.

Ella held on for dear life, screaming at the top of her lungs as the flying dinosaur zoomed over the steaming piles of rubbish, with his tongue flopping merrily out of his mouth. He was always happiest when he was in the air, even if it was while weaving through wafts of Whiffington's waste.

'I can't look! Tell me when we land! We are going to land, right? Are we there yet?' Ella spluttered nervously as she squeezed her eyes tightly shut.

It was a shame that Ella wasn't looking, because she would have seen the most wonderful magic happening around her! Brilliant bursts of blue light shot out of the

ELLA AND THE ELVES

Christmasaurus's icy spines, causing the world around
them to blur into a distant blip. Then, in a whirl that
went from brightest cobalt to deepest aquamarine and
back again, they travelled to a far-off place. No scientific
theory or mathematical equation could have explained
it. It was beyond the law of time; this was the law of
Christmas time! When Ella finally opened her
eyes again, she discovered that they were soaring over
the snowy glaciers of the North Pole.

'What . . . How did . . . Where . . . ?' Ella had so many questions! But, before she could settle on which one to ask, the Christmasaurus spiralled down towards a big empty nothing and landed in a wide-open expanse of snow.

'I hate FLYING!' Ella shrieked as she slid off the Christmasaurus's back and kissed the snow. 'Next time you've got to give a girl a little warning before you take off into the sky! Where are we, anyway?'

Ella turned a full circle, scanning her surroundings for a clue. Then, finding nothing but snow as far as the eye could see, she spun back to where she'd started – only to discover that her new dinosaur companion had totally vanished.

'Erm . . . Hello?' she called.

Nothing.

'Very funny, Mr Dinosaur . . . creature . . . thing!'

Still nothing.

As Ella stood in the middle of the snow, surrounded by nothing but snow, the clouds overhead began to steadily cover her in . . . you guessed it, snow!

'I'm serious! You can't whisk me into the sky unexpectedly and drop me in the middle of –'

POP!

The Christmasaurus appeared again in front of her like a bubble in reverse.

'How did you do that?' Ella gasped.

The Christmasaurus stepped aside, revealing something red and white and rather delicious-looking sticking out of the snow.

'Is that a candy cane?' Ella asked, her tummy growling so fiercely that even the Christmasaurus heard it as he bowed his head for Ella to take the treat.

'Now, this is WAY better than sprouts!' She grinned, dropping to her knees and crunching the swirly stick of yumminess.

'Hey, there's writing in the middle,' Ella mumbled through a mouthful of the most delicious, minty candy

247

cane she'd ever tasted. As she peered at the tiny letters that ran through the centre, she saw they spelt her name:

ELLA NOYING

'That's cool – it says my name inside!' Ella said, but when she looked up again she froze in total shock. The delicious candy cane had worked its delicious magic and revealed the hidden world of Christmas to Ella.

'Dino, I've a feeling we're not in Whiffington any more.' Ella rubbed her eyes to check if she was really seeing what she thought she was seeing – the tiny elf village; the toboggan run with a loop-the-loop; snowmen ice skating on a frozen outdoor swimming pool; a polar bear playing carols on a xylophone made of icicles; chimneys billowing smoke that smelt of mince pies; and candy canes as tall as trees.

'This is . . . it's . . .' Ella knew exactly where she was, as any child would, but for some reason she couldn't seem to say it, so the Christmasaurus just nodded excitedly.

'**NO WAY!** This is so amazing! I mean, this is literally *the* coolest day **EV-ER**! I've always dreamt of exploring the North Pole! Oh my goodness, I can't wait to tell Lucy and Norman about this. They will be

SO jealous! Ah man, I don't have a camera. Is Santa here? Can we see him? Are there elves here? Tell me there are elves here! I want to meet an elf. Can I keep an elf? OK, maybe not permanently, but maybe just for a week?'

'Keep an elf? Did you hear that?
An elf is not a dog or cat!'

sang a tuneful voice from behind them, making Ella leap out of her skin.

'Who's there?!' she squeaked, spinning round to see no one. Then she heard someone clear their throat somewhere near her feet, and her jaw dropped as she looked down to find eight small, merry faces staring up at her.

'We are eight of Santa's elves.
Please, let us introduce ourselves . . .'

And suddenly the eight creatures began performing a little song and dance.

'We're Snowcrumb, Spudcheeks and Sparklefoot,
I'm Starlump and that's Sugarsnout.
My name's Snozzletrump and he's called
    Specklehump.
And, last but not least, he's Sprout!'

Ella started clapping, but the elves' performance had
only just begun . . .

ELLA AND THE ELVES

'We're mining elves of the Northern Realm,
And digging for toys is our duty.
Every member will dig all December
To harvest a sleighful of booty.
We sing while we dig and dig while we sing
To help pass the time on our mission.
For every elf, even those on the shelf,
Is a most underrated musician.
Now we've paused for a song, we must
   move along.
There's plenty of digging to do.
So, tell us your name and we'll be on our way
To dig up a toy just for you!'

Ella was about to explode into applause, for it truly was
a magical performance. But her heart sank deep in her
chest at the realization that she didn't belong there.

   'What's the matter? You look so sad.
   Was our singing really that bad?'

asked a very concerned Starlump.

'Oh, no! Not at all. Your singing was wonderful. It's just –' Ella gulped – 'you won't be digging up any toys for me. I found out tonight that I'm on . . . the *Naughty List*.'

If there was such a thing as tumbleweed in the North Pole, it would have blown across the snow between them as the eight elves silently gawped at the Naughty Lister in front of them.

> 'The North Pole is a secret.
> People don't know we exist,
> So we don't get many guests
> Especially from the Naughty List,'

explained Starlump kindly, reaching up to stroke Ella's hand.

The Christmasaurus started roaring and groaning, huffing hot air out of his nostrils as though passionately speaking to the elves. It made no sense to Ella at all, but the elves seemed to know exactly what this strange dinosaur was saying.

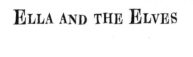

'So the reason you're on the Naughty List
Can be found inside your bag?
But we're warned that if we open it
The contents will make us gag!'

sang Specklehump, but the Christmasaurus knew that curiosity would get the better of the elves and they would not be able to resist . . .

PUFF!

They unzipped Ella's bag, and a cloud of green sprout gas was released, giving the crowd of elves a face-full of rotten air! They coughed and spluttered and fell about in utter disgust.

'It smells like swamp! It smells like nappies!
My nostrils are in so much pain!
What in the world is this gross pile of green?
Tell us, Ella, does it have a name?'

Ella reached into her bag and pulled out one of her mother's grotesque green balls of grot and held it in the air for all to see.

'These, my new elf friends, are a British Christmas tradition. While Americans eat sweet fruitcake, and the Italians munch warm panettone, once a year we try our best to gulp down the dreaded Brussels sprout!'

The elves looked at each other with a mixture of fear and disgust.

'You poor child, that's revolting!
No wonder you can't eat it!
What can we do? How can we help?
It's evil – we must defeat it!'

the elves chanted determinedly.

The Christmasaurus roared with delight and this gang of impossible creatures huddled together and began hatching a plan.

A few moments later, they turned to Ella with serious looks on their faces.

'There's only one elf who can save this disaster.
These Brussels sprouts need to be seen
By our legendary, masterful, wizened elf-chef,
So we'll take you to meet Buttercream.'

CHAPTER TWENTY-SIX
THE SNOW RANCH

The festive gang and their secret visitor began their journey through the North Pole, keeping to the shadows and avoiding the bustling streets of Elfville, which were alive with Christmas preparations.

There were so many bizarre, magical things for Ella to see, and she wished she could just stop and watch for a while to take it all in, particularly the creatures. Some she recognized from Christmas cards, like the elves and the reindeer galloping across the distant sky, but there were also creatures she'd never seen anywhere in the world before . . .

Like the **DECEMBER WHALE**, which can hold its breath for eleven months and only surfaces in December at the North Pole to feed on the leftover cuttings of gingerbread dough.

Or the **SORE-NOSED TWINKLE**, which is about the size of a mouse and hangs from Christmas trees by its nose, twinkling like starlight. Unfortunately, its nose, what with it being twice as long as its body, has a painful tendency to be trodden on by elves.

Then there were **GRUMPETS**, foul-tempered boglins that occupy the nooks and crannies of elf dwellings to shelter from the snow, which they despise and are constantly at battle with . . .

FAIRY MITES, tiny bugs with glowing bottoms, which they use to camouflage themselves among fairy lights. Not to be confused with . . .

TINSEL BEETLES, which are actually very useful bugs to have around at Christmas as their bristly legs clean the tinsel they nest in.

There was a flock of **TONE-DEAF JINGLES**, a type of parrot that squawks a tune so hideous it can shatter the thickest ice.

Also, **WREATH WORMS**, green worms found in the ice that the elves like to hang on their doors as festive wreaths . . . until the worm gets bored and slithers away.

And **CAROLLING RACOONS**, mischievous critters that mimic Christmas carollers to tempt people to their front doors so they can sneak inside in search of treats.

There were so many amazing sights and sounds that Ella's heart felt full to bursting with the magic of it all. But then, as a reindeer galloped through the sky over the group of elves and the Christmasaurus, and everyone stopped dead-still hoping it didn't see them, tears began to brim in Ella's eyes as a thought popped into her head and wouldn't get out.

'I'm not even supposed to be here, am I? That's why we're sneaking about, right? Why would Santa want someone on the Naughty List in the North Pole?'

The Christmasaurus shook his head and gave her a comforting nudge with his scaly nose. Then the elves began singing in hushed voices.

'Santa's not allowed to know.
He can't find out you're here.
He'll try to change the Naughty List,
But mustn't interfere.
He's just supposed to give the gifts,
Nothing more or less,
But he's so jolly, nice and kind
He really is the best.
He's like a giant puppy,
He can't resist temptation
To give a child a present
Whatever their reputation,
But it's against the Santa Oath.

He's not allowed to help
Children leap from list to list,
But we're not him – we're elves!
So we can give a gentle nudge
To help you cross the line
From Naughty List to Nice List,
And all in song and rhyme!'

Ella smiled and felt all her worries melt away for a moment, like she'd just had a gulp of hot chocolate.

'Well, when it comes to sneaking around at night, I am the master,' she joked, with a sad smile. But, as the Christmasaurus led the way through the snow, Ella saw her path to the Nice List appear before her in the footprints he left behind, and she decided there and then that her sneaking-out days were over – even if it meant having to eat terrible vegetables!

They crept round the back of the reindeer stables and stayed under the cover of the pine trees along the edge of the Forest of Wishes, until they were slap-bang in front of the grandest log cabin your brain could possibly imagine.

Fancy giving it a go?
OK, here goes!

Imagine a really tiny, unthinkably plain, snoringly boring, utterly ordinary log cabin, with one teeny window and an even teenier door. Inside there's only one bedroom, and it smells like sweaty feet on a hot day.

Got it? Good.

Oh, did I forget to mention that it's OPPOSITES DAY? Take everything you just imagined and flip it!

Santa's Snow Ranch was so gobsmackingly grand and magical that Ella had no words to say except:

'Please tell me we're going in there!'

She pointed at the polar-bear-sized front doors.

The Christmasaurus shook his head – *not in there.*

He raised his chin towards the top of the Snow Ranch, indicating a tall tower that Ella thought would have been more at home on a fairy-tale castle than a log cabin, and there, at the very top of the tower, was a window and a warm glow flickering within.

'Up there?' Ella asked excitedly.

261

The Christmasaurus nodded, crouching down for her to climb aboard.

'Are you coming?' Ella asked her elf escorts.

> 'Us? Fly? You must be joking.
> We're terrified of heights!
> We much prefer the stairs,
> However many flights.
> We have a cunning plan
> We're putting into action –
> You fly up to the reading room
> And we'll cause a distraction!
> It's been so good to meet you,
> Now hold on to the Christmasaurus
> And if you're caught by Santa Claus
> Don't tell him that you saw us!'

The elves finished their song with a deep bow, and the Christmasaurus leapt into the sky, climbing up the side of the grand Snow Ranch until they were hovering silently just outside the window of the warm, glowing room and, as Ella peeped inside, she caught sight of something moving within.

Or not *something* but **SOMEONE.**

Someone who was larger than life, dressed in a shimmering, deep red onesie and dunking crumpets into what looked like a mug of custard.

Now of course Ella had never met him before, but she knew in an instant that there was only one person this could be. And, even though she knew she was very much NOT supposed to be seen by this specific person, being so close to a LEGEND meant that Ella found herself unable to stop herself . . .

'Santa!'

she blurted OUT LOUD, causing the magical man to swivel round in his chair and face them.

'Pluck my turkey! Who the jingle is out there?' Santa boomed and, just like that, the game was up.

CHAPTER TWENTY-SEVEN

BUTTERCREAM

S anta threw back the curtains and poked his nose out into the frosty North Pole air.

'Hello?' he called, but he heard nothing but his own booming voice echo back from across the empty sky.

HELLO. HELLO. Hello.

'How very peculiar. I could have sworn I heard someone call my name.' He scratched his snow-white beard.

Now, I bet you're wondering where Ella and the Christmasaurus disappeared to, right? Well, they didn't disappear at all! In fact, if Santa had only glanced *up* instead of *out*, he would have discovered that they were hovering just above his head, trying their best not to make a noise. Not to move. Not even to breathe!

'*Santa!*' came a distant call, this time from somewhere within the Snow Ranch and in perfect elf-harmony.

'What do those pesky elves want now? Can't a jolly fella get a minute's peace without someone bursting into a song and dance? Just a moment to himself to enjoy a crumpet or three with his toes nice and toasty by the fire.'

**'Santa, Santa! Please come quick!
Sound the warning trumpet!'**

the elves belted, sounding closer now, and Ella could make out the distinct tones of Snozzletrump, Sparklefoot, Specklehump, Sugarsnout, Starlump, Snowcrumb, Spudcheeks and, not forgetting, Sprout.

'Warning trumpet? Well, Kringle my Krampus,

this had better not be just another grumpet stuck in a chimney or I'll . . .'

'Santa, we have awful news!
The kitchen's out of crumpets!'

the elves bellowed as Ella heard them burst into the room. **'OUT OF CRUMPETS!'**

Santa boomed, turning away from the window to face the elves. 'What a disaster! I couldn't have eaten that many . . . could I?'

The Christmasaurus slowly and carefully floated down low enough to peer into the room without being seen, and they saw Santa striding out of the door, determined to get to the bottom of this crumpet disaster. The eight elves followed at his heels, trying their hardest not to giggle.

The moment they were gone, the Christmasaurus flew into the room and Ella jumped down.

'That was Santa. The *actual* Santa. THE Santa!' Ella whispered, still totally mesmerized by the magical man.

The Christmasaurus nodded, but there was no time to waste. They didn't have long and those sprouts in Ella's bag needed help immediately. He pulled open the drawer in Santa's desk, revealing the important-looking, red telephone, and gave a gentle roar.

'Who are we calling?' Ella asked as she picked up the receiver. The Christmasaurus used his snout to push the single button, which was a direct line to . . .

> 'Buttercream here, how can I help you?
> Would you like me to read the room-service
> menu?'

sang a cheerful voice down the line.

The Christmasaurus replied with frantic **roars** and **growls** that the elf on the other end of the line had no trouble deciphering.

> 'Cold, bitter sprouts? Blergh, I feel a little sick.
> Stay where you are – I'll be there in a tick!'

the elf sang and by the time Ella had hung up the telephone there was a **KNOCK!** **KNOCK!** at the door.

Ella opened it carefully, and in waltzed Buttercream pushing her mobile kitchen trolley.

'Show me the spouts, show me the greens!
Let's turn them into the veg of your dreams.'

the elf chimed merrily as she adjusted the apron around her waist and rolled up her sleeves, ready for action. Ella held her breath and unzipped her backpack.

'Well, bless my baubles, that's quite a pong!
This recipe's gone very wrong!
But not to worry – we'll take a look
In my magical vegetable recipe book.'

Buttercream trilled, and slid a glimmering green book out from her kitchen trolley.

'Did she say *magical* recipe book?' Ella whispered to

the Christmasaurus, who nodded excitedly, watching the tiny chef flick through the pages.

> 'Sauerkraut, Savoy cabbage, Spinach . . .
> **SPROUT!**
> **Stand back! Let's sort these offenders out . . .'**

Buttercream flung the doors of her trolley open, and Ella watched in awe as it magically grew bigger and folded out in seemingly impossible ways, taking up more and more space in the cosy reading room. There were shelves and drawers for every pot and pan an elf could ever need. There were cupboards full of contraptions like whisks, blenders, sieves, measuring cups, pie pans, pastry bags, rolling pins, a fully stocked spice rack, a small herb garden, a toaster, a grill, a microwave and practically everything Ella had ever seen in all the kitchens she'd ever been in.

'How did that fit in there?' Ella gawped in amazement.

The Christmasaurus shrugged. There were lots of inexplicable, seemingly undoable, should-be-impossible things in the North Pole and he had learnt that trying

to figure out how they work just makes your head hurt. It was best to trust the magic and not worry about questions that had no answers.

    'Well, what are you waiting for?
    Don't stand there looking!
    It's always faster with two people cooking!'

Buttercream said, turning the recipe book to face Ella.

'Er . . . I'm really not a very good cook!' Ella said nervously.

**'It's easy-peasy! Anyone can cook.
Just do what it says inside this book!'**

And, with that, they set to work together to rescue the spoiled sprouts. They poured them into a large mixing bowl.

DONG! DONG! DONG!

Ella did as the recipe said and added a glug of tangy balsamic vinegar and a spoonful of sweet maple syrup, while Buttercream climbed up a little stepladder to add two elf-handfuls of salt. Then they pan-fried the sprouts with garlic until they were golden and crispy around the edges, ready to plate-up and sprinkle with some fresh, sweet pomegranate seeds.

'Are you sure about this? I mean, vinegar and syrup, sprouts and pomegranate . . . It's a bit of a mish-mash of flavours,' Ella said.

BUTTERCREAM

Buttercream said nothing and simply handed Ella a fork.

'OK, here goes!' Ella gulped and nervously popped the sprout into her mouth.

Well, the taste that Ella experienced was like nothing she'd ever had before.

'It's sweet and salty . . . and crispy and juicy at the same time. It's like eating chips and sweets together. These sprouts are

THE BEST THING
I'VE EVER EATEN!'

Ella cried with joy, and she plunged her fork back in for a second and third and fourth and fifth helping . . . until the bowl was empty!

'I can't wait to show my mum that recipe. It'll blow her mind!' Ella said, rubbing her happy, full tummy. 'Wait – if you can do that with sprouts, can you make other vegetables taste that amazing too?'

'Why, of course I can, and so can you!
This book will show you what to do.'

And Buttercream closed the glistening green recipe book and handed it to Ella.

'It's full of recipes from across the planet.
So, if you liked sprouts and pomegranate,
You'll love each and every dish.
They're good for you and SO delish!
So, why not cook them with your mummy?
For two chefs make food twice as yummy!'

Ella took the book from the elf. The thought of being able to cook things at home that tasted as incredible as the food she'd eaten in the North Pole was enough to make her tummy rumble in excitement, but even better would be being able to share them with her mum!

'Thank you so much!' Ella said, and she pulled Buttercream in for a big squishy hug, which was interrupted (to Buttercream's relief!) by a thundering

BOOM! BOOM! BOOM!

'Santa's coming! Time to go!
Your secret's safe – he'll never know.
Now fly away, on the double,
And let cooking keep you out of trouble.'

As Buttercream spun round, she waved her whisk in the air like a wand, causing her kitchen trolley to fold back in on itself, packing everything perfectly into the tiny trolley for the elf to push out of the door. Ella jumped on to the Christmasaurus's back with the magical recipe book tucked under her arm.

'What a relief! Crumpet crisis averted!' they heard Santa grumbling to himself as he climbed the stairs. 'I knew we'd have some crumpets stashed away somewhere. Silly elves, they can find a toy under a snowfield in the middle of a blizzard but can't spot a crumpet in a bread bin.'

The Christmasaurus leapt out of the window and

disappeared into the sky, whizzing Ella back home just in time to greet the sunrise as she climbed in through her bedroom window and slid into bed.

❄

Later that very same day, Ella came home from school full of energy and excitement.

'Mum, grab your apron,' she yelled, running upstairs to her room.

'What did you say?'

'I said, "Grab your apron" – let's cook!' Ella called, rushing back down to the kitchen.

'Oh, Ella, what a surprise! I knew you'd get the cooking bug eventually; it runs in the family. Now, there's a stewed spinach recipe I had my eye on . . .' Mrs Noying began flicking through the stained pages of her old cookbook.

'Actually, I thought we could try something from this recipe book,' Ella said, handing her mum Buttercream's gloriously shiny green book.

'Well, I've never seen any of these recipes before,' Mrs Noying said, flicking through its contents suspiciously. 'Where did it come from?'

BUTTERCREAM

'You wouldn't believe me if I told you.'

'Try me.'

'A dinosaur flew me to the North Pole last night, and an elf gave me that book,' Ella said, as though it were the most normal thing in the world.

Mrs Noying stared at her daughter for a moment then burst out laughing.

'Well, if your cooking is as creative as your imagination, then we'll be in for a real tasty treat. Let's give it a whirl.'

Without any hesitation, they both threw on their aprons and began making the scrummiest, most veg-tastic creations that would have made Buttercream proud.

The Christmasaurus gazed through the kitchen window as the Noying family sat down to dinner. He couldn't help but smile as, for the first time in a long time, Ella didn't need to secretly scrape the food into her bag. Even Mr Noying asked for a second helping!

'This is . . . DELICIOUS!'

he cheered. 'You've done it!'

THE CHRISTMASAURUS AND THE NAUGHTY LIST

'Well, I couldn't have done it without Ella. She's a natural chef!' Mrs Noying beamed with pride, and a soft glow emitted from within the Naughty List as Ella's name faded away. She had no intention of ever sneaking out of her house ever again!

The Christmasaurus scooped up the Naughty List and launched into the evening air like a rocket, ready for his next Naughty List mission.

CHAPTER TWENTY-EIGHT
GEMOLINA SHINE

Gemolina Shine was going to be a star. There was no doubt about it. It was that simple. She just knew she was born to be on stage in front of thousands of adoring fans cheering her name while she sang and danced.

She was going to live in a twenty-storey mansion in the Hollywood Hills when she was being a movie star, then whizz across to New York on her private jet when she wanted to star on Broadway. And that's without even mentioning her endless discography of multi-platinum-selling albums, the billions and billions of streams or the cabinets full of awards!

Yes, Gemolina was destined to be BIG!!

BUT that life was still a long way away, because right now Gemolina was still only eleven years old.

She was off to a pretty good start, though. You see, ever since she could walk and talk, Gemolina had been centre stage.

'Dance for us, little Gemstone,' cooed her mumsy.

'Sing us a song, Gem-gem!' Her daddy smiled, and they clicked record on the camcorder (that's like a super-old-fashioned video camera . . . which is basically like a really big version of the camera app on your phone). Gemolina never missed an opportunity to show off her talents. With a big toothy smile on her face, she'd sing this and that, dance here and there, spinning around the living room so fast and with such enthusiasm that she burnt holes in the carpet! And, even when the whole room was full of grey smoke, she would twirl through it like a popstar through dry ice in a music video.

It wasn't long before Gemolina started to crave being in front of the camera ALL THE TIME!

'Film me, Mumsy!'

she demanded as she performed *Les Misérables* in its entirety in their living room at age five.

'Record this, Daddy!'

she insisted as she danced *Swan Lake* in the kitchen while his breakfast got cold.

And, even though she desperately wished to be on TV when she grew up, Gemolina hated nothing more than when all the grown-ups were sat in the living room looking at the screen when they could have been watching her!

'WATCH ME!
WATCH ME!
WATCH ME!'

she would whine to her parents constantly.

Gemolina didn't have any brothers or sisters, which

meant she was ALWAYS the centre of attention. There was no one to steal her toys. No one to eat the biggest slice of pizza. No one to tell her to stop being such a show-off! Being the centre of attention was where Gemolina felt most at home, so even when she was at school surrounded by dozens of other kids, she still expected everyone to focus on *her*.

The problem was that Gemolina wasn't very good at most school subjects, so she had to come up with inventive ways to make sure everyone was paying attention to her and no one else.

She was miserable at maths, until she dreamt up **MATHS: THE MUSICAL!** – a tap-dancing journey through the times tables, which Gemolina spontaneously performed on the desks, thereby totally ruining everyone else's work.

She wasn't particularly swotty at science, until she came up with **SCIENCE SPECTACULAR!** – an experimental song and dance exploration of the periodic table, which resulted in numerous smashed test tubes and some unplanned pyrotechnics from the Bunsen burners.

She managed to transform PE into a parade, geography into a rock concert, and history into a dramatic re-enactment of the monumental moment she discovered *she* could sing, which was definitely not part of the curriculum.

She turned every school event into *Gemolina Shine moments*. Like sports day, when she decided to pirouette the one-hundred-metre race instead of running, so despite coming last *she* got a standing ovation from the crowd and not Sam Bell (who actually won).

Wherever Gemolina Shine went, she made it

ALL ABOUT HER!

Which is why it should be no surprise that her favourite subject was the one where she knew she would always be centre stage: PERFORMING ARTS!

From the moment she exploded into the school theatre, Gemolina transformed into what she liked to call *superstar mode*. She was no longer plain old Gemolina from South Boringville on Planet Nowhere. Oh no. When she was in performing arts class, she was Gemolina – future superstar of the world!

Gemolina had no desire to share the limelight with anyone, and the other kids didn't stand a chance at getting the solos, the lead roles – or sometimes any roles at all for that matter!

'Today we're going to be looking at a musical called

Cats!' Mrs Symphony, their performing arts teacher, had declared one day.

'Say no more! And a *five, six, seven, eight* . . .' Gemolina counted herself in, and a one-girl performance of *Cats* began. Gemolina pranced into every part, knew the lyrics and danced all the steps. She even served the snacks in the interval, and two hours later the class left the school theatre in a bit of a daze – not surprising given that the lesson was only supposed to be forty-five minutes long!

You know your school shows? The ones where your parents get all excited and dress up in their going-out clothes just to sit in those uncomfortable seats? The ones where if they need to pee, they just have to cross their legs and hold it, in case they miss their child say the two words they've been given? Yeah, those school shows. Well, Gemolina put all her focus into making sure that *she* got the starring role, no matter what.

In the school production of *Annie*, she played Annie. When they did *Beauty and the Beast*, she played Beauty AND the Beast (yes, both of them. Best not to ask how . . .).

The biggest and most important school show of the year was always the Christmas concert, which was the kick-off event for the final weeks of term that were full of Christmas fun. The most important part of the most important show was THE CHRISTMAS SOLO! It was the gift of Christmas song from the school to the parents, where just one student would sing while the school Christmas lights were switched on.

It was a school tradition, and Christmas didn't truly begin until that solo had been sung.

Each year a piece of paper was pinned on the school noticeboard for anyone interested in auditioning to write their name on. The list of names of people used to span two whole pages, but that changed when Gemolina joined the school. Now the solo always seemed to be given to her, so everyone else stopped bothering to even audition. What was the point?!

But that was about to change . . .

It was the first week of December, and Gemolina pranced through school as though she was on camera, swishing her hair like a shampoo advert and humming loudly enough for everyone to hear just how pitch-perfect she was, when she suddenly stopped in her tracks like she'd run into an invisible forcefield.

The sign-up sheet had caught her eye, stunning her into silence. Yesterday, when she had written her name (in glittering gold ink, naturally, and so big that it took up most of the page), everything had been fine. Normal. But now, there, just beneath Gemolina's name, was something awful, something shocking, something so totally hideous that Gemolina could hardly believe what she was seeing.

It was SOMEONE ELSE'S NAME.

Someone else who thought they had a shot at the Christmas solo.

But who could this potential show-stealer be? No one had ever dared to even attempt to claim the spotlight from Gemolina Shine.

Gemolina marched up to it and read the name out loud in a dramatic whisper worthy of an Academy Award: **'DOROTHY DORKINS!'**

CHAPTER TWENTY-NINE
WHATEVER IT TAKES

What Gemolina did next was rotten. What Gemolina did next was mean. What Gemolina did next was classic Naughty List behaviour.

It was the following Monday: AUDITION DAY. The day when Mrs Symphony and a selection of staff would sit behind a table in the auditorium doing their best Simon Cowell impressions, eating chocolate Bourbons and drinking stinky coffee while watching the students try their best to win that coveted Christmas solo spot! For the last few years, the teachers had done this just for show, because Gemolina had been the

ONLY one who put herself forward, so this year Mrs Symphony and the other teachers were excited to be auditioning someone else!

Gemolina arrived earlier than usual to make sure that she was the first one seen. Her plan was to set the bar so impossibly high that Dorothy Dorkins would never be able to reach it.

I mean, who even is this Dorothy Dorkins? Gemolina thought. *I'm sure she's that girl who sits in the corner of every lesson, hardly ever saying a word to anyone. When has she ever showed any interest in singing? Who does she think she is?!*

But Gemolina was in for surprise. When she walked backstage at the school auditorium, she found that Dorothy Dorkins had already arrived!

There Dorothy was, sitting quietly with her hands on her knees, looking at the ground.

Gemolina's blood was boiling. Nobody auditioned before *she* did!

Then she took a deep breath.

Don't let it throw you, Gem-gem. You're a star, you're a star, you're a star, Gemolina recited to herself in her head as she threw off her school bag and started warming up in the tiny dressing room. She flung herself dramatically this way, before launching that way, twirling around like a ballerina.

'Don't mind if I warm up, do you?' Gemolina asked, as she high-kicked her way over to where Dorothy was sitting. She was sure this would intimidate her enemy.

'No,' Dorothy whispered.

'Aren't *you* going to warm up?'

'No, I don't think so. I've never really warmed up before. I've never auditioned for anything before actually, so I'm not really sure what I'm doing,' Dorothy confessed nervously.

Gemolina gave a sickly smile. 'Well, no one ever gets their first audition except me, but it's sweet of you to try.'

'**DOROTHY DORKINS!**' Mrs Symphony called from within the auditorium. 'You're up!'

'Good luck,' Gemolina called as Dorothy stood to go to her audition.

'I thought it was bad luck to say that in a theatre?' Dorothy asked, looking a little concerned.

'Oh, yes . . . I forgot. Well, I guess we'll find out if

the superstition is true!' said Gemolina, who knew full well that you're meant to say 'break a leg' to an actor, NEVER 'good luck'!

Dorothy nervously edged her way into the auditorium and the door closed behind her, leaving Gemolina alone.

She doesn't stand a chance. Gemolina smiled, then started to warm up her voice by making all sorts of strange sounds. 'Me-me-me, ma-ma-ma, mo-mo-ERGH!'

Gemolina's voice suddenly wobbled and cracked. It never did that unless she was nervous, and she NEVER got nervous at auditions!

'Me-me-me, ma-ma-ma, mo-mo-ERGH!'

293

Her voice croaked again. Her heart sank. This could not be happening. Not today.

She started to worry. *What if my voice does that during my audition?*

She started to panic. *What if Dorothy is a better singer than me?*

Then: *What if I don't get the Christmas solo?* Gemolina suddenly felt as though the walls were closing in around her and there was no way out. She had to do something to make sure she was the one to get the solo.

The tinkling of piano music floated from inside the auditorium. Dorothy was about to sing! She was about to steal Gemolina's solo.

NOT TODAY! Gemolina thought, and without hesitation she did something utterly awful. Totally terrible. Stupendously spiteful. She set off the fire alarm!

HONK HONK HONK!
HONK HONK HONK!

WHATEVER IT TAKES

The warning sound was deafening as it blasted throughout the school theatre. The emergency lighting kicked in too, flashing blinding blue lights around the hallways and the auditorium. But worst of all were the sprinklers.

Jets of ice-cold water gushed from the ceiling of the auditorium, giving everyone inside a most unpleasant shower. Needless to say, Dorothy Dorkins' audition was over before it had even begun as she ran to the wings to take cover and the teachers rushed to save their Bourbon biscuits from going soggy.

Suddenly the doors to the auditorium burst open and Gemolina exploded into the theatre with a huge, cheesy grin plastered over her face.

'Gemolina, what are you doing? We need to evacuate the building!' called Mrs Symphony through the heavy indoor shower.

But Gemolina wasn't going anywhere. She pulled an umbrella out of nowhere, then started singing.

'I'm singin' in the rain,
Just singin' in the rain . . .'

She skipped merrily down the aisle of the theatre, then climbed across the soggy seats until she was at the judges' table, singing **LOUDLY** in their faces so they could hear her above the fire alarm.

With the blue emergency lighting as her spotlight and the sprinkler shower as her backdrop, Gemolina tap-danced across the table and up to the stage, throwing a very soggy Dorothy Dorkins a wink before hitting her big final note just as the fire alarm stopped screeching.

Whatever It Takes

The dripping water rapped down like a rapturous applause, and the teachers looked totally dumbfounded by what they had just seen.

'Sorry,' Gemolina huffed, out of breath from her performance. 'I just . . . saw the rain and improvised.'

'Very impressive, Gemolina. I don't think we need to see any more today,' said Mrs Symphony.

'But . . . I didn't get a chance to sing,' called Dorothy from the wings.

'Oh, Dorothy! I totally forgot about you! Yes, you're right – it's only fair you get another chance. We'll see you again tomorrow. Thank you both for coming in today. It was a false alarm, so back to class now.'

Gemolina and Dorothy walked out of the soaking wet theatre together.

'I wonder why the sprinklers went off when there's no fire,' Dorothy said as they squelched along the corridor to maths.

'I guess it is bad luck to say "good luck" after all,' Gemolina said with a shrug, as though she were as confused as Dorothy about the whole thing.

297

'Well, at least I can try again tomorrow,' said a deflated Dorothy, sighing.

'Yes, good luck!' Gemolina grinned as they took their seats in maths. She spent the whole lesson coming up with her plan to sabotage Dorothy's next audition.

The next day, Dorothy was ready to put the disaster of her last audition behind her and to give it her all – this time with no alarms or sprinklers.

And she was right.

This time there would be no alarm or sprinklers. This time there would be something **WORSE!**

Each class at school had its own Class Pet. There was everything including tiny little hamsters, goldfish and even an enormous chicken – Gemolina had spent all morning secretly collecting them ALL from the classrooms. Just as Dorothy stepped out into the spotlight, Gemolina released them from the shadows on to the stage!

Gerbils and mice poured from stage left; guinea pigs and hamsters leapt in from stage right, in what looked like a very expensive production of *Dr Dolittle*. A whole petting zoo's worth of rodents that were usually tucked

WHATEVER IT TAKES

up in hutches and cages in the classrooms were now scattering across the stage in the middle of poor Dorothy's audition!

SQUEAK! SQUEAK! SQUEEEEEEEEAK!

The rodents suddenly dived off the stage and into the auditorium, sending the teachers running for cover.

'Sorry, Dorothy, let's try one more time tomorrow!

ARRRGHHHH!'

screamed Mrs Symphony as she leapt on to the table, away from a rather peckish mouse from Year Two that was after her toes.

'OK,' said Dorothy, slumping.

Tomorrow soon came around, and this time Dorothy was sure that absolutely nothing could go wrong.

Think again, Dorothy!

As the soft piano started tinkling its beautiful introduction to Dorothy's audition song, there was an almighty racket from outside.

BANG! CRASH!

TOOT! TOOT!

'What on earth is that noise?' cried Mrs Symphony.

The theatre doors burst open and in came the school marching band in a long parade that led them up to the stage.

'What on earth are you doing here?' screamed Mrs Symphony once the band had stopped marching.

'Practising,' said the bandmaster.

'But don't you usually practise in the sports hall?'

'Yes, but we received a note from Principal McGilly to say that we'd been moved to the theatre today.' The bandmaster handed the note over to Mrs Symphony.

Gemolina was watching all this with a knot in her tummy, hoping, pleading, praying that Mrs Symphony wouldn't notice the **FAKED HANDWRITING!**

That's right! You read that correctly: Gemolina had **FORGED** the headmaster's handwriting to move the marching band into the theatre!

Mrs Symphony sighed. 'I wasn't made aware of this.'

'Neither were we. Top idea, though – much better acoustics in here. And a one, two, three, four!' he counted the band in.

BOOM! BOOM! BOOM!

went the big bass drum.

CRASH! CRASH! CRASH!

smashed the cymbals as they all marched around the stage.

'I think we'd better . . .' Mrs Symphony began.

'Try tomorrow?' Dorothy finished for her, having to yell to be heard over the noise.

WHATEVER IT TAKES

'Exactly!'

Dorothy sighed. The concert was in two days' time, which meant that tomorrow would be her last chance! It felt hopeless!

But, luckily for her, just before Dorothy's next audition, a very special dinosaur who was about to change everything appeared outside the school theatre.

CHAPTER THIRTY
A SINGING TORNADO

The swirly-twirly whirlpool of light that had brought the Christmasaurus to the school had only just vanished when a soft scuffing of footsteps on the gravel path caught his ear. He quickly dived to hide in a nearby bush, narrowly avoiding being seen by a nervous little girl heading inside for her last chance at claiming the school's singing solo.

Leaving the Naughty List safely hidden in the bush, the Christmasaurus quietly crept after her. *Could this timid little girl who was nervously biting her lip be his Naughty Lister?* he wondered. But his thoughts were soon corrected by a snort of giggles coming from the back of the theatre.

The dinosaur crouched as low as he could and crawled along the carpet until he was in the row of seats directly behind the giggling culprit: Gemolina. She was hidden in the shadows and had something in her hand that looked like a large TV remote.

'OK then, Dorothy. Let's give this one last try, shall we? The Christmas concert is tomorrow night, so this is our last chance to decide who will be singing the solo. Good luck,' said Mrs Symphony from behind the judges' table. She and all the other teachers sat with umbrellas and ear defenders at the ready, their eyes scanning for rodents. They were taking no chances today!

Dorothy's eyes widened at hearing the unlucky words!

'Oh, I beg your pardon. I mean, *break a leg*!' Mrs Symphony corrected, seeing the look on Dorothy's face. But was it too late? Had the damage been done?

The piano started. Nothing awful yet.

Dorothy took a breath . . . still nothing. So far so good.

She opened her mouth to sing, and at that very moment the Christmasaurus saw Gemolina press a button on the remote control in her hand.

CLANK!

A loud mechanical sound came from somewhere beneath the stage, and then the whole floor under Dorothy's feet started to rotate and move, turning her round until she was facing the back of the stage.

Dorothy was standing on a revolving floor, and Gemolina had the controls!

Gemolina could hardly suppress the giggling as she pressed START then STOP, START then STOP on the remote control, whizzing Dorothy round.

'Sorry about that, Dorothy. Must be a little malfunction,' Mrs Symphony said. 'Still, the show must go on. Do keep going!'

Dorothy opened her mouth to sing, but Gemolina

pressed the button, sending the stage spinning again! This time, she didn't stop it. She just let poor Dorothy spin round and round until she looked like a singing tornado. Dorothy dropped to her knees and tried to hold on, but the stage was getting faster and faster. She wouldn't be able to hold on much longer!

'Take cover!' Mrs Symphony cried, sensing what was about to happen, and the teachers ducked under the judges' table as poor Dorothy was sent flying over their heads, across the theatre and out through the doors.

Job done, thought Gemolina, smiling to herself. That solo was hers! But, as she turned to pack the remote control into her school bag, she discovered that she wasn't the only one hiding at the back of the theatre.

CHAPTER THIRTY-ONE

ENCORE

Gemolina saw feet. Gemolina saw claws. Gemolina saw teeth. Gemolina saw jaws!

She was so totally terrified of the prehistoric creature before her that she couldn't even bring herself to scream, which was handy really as it would have absolutely blown her cover!

So Gemolina ran as fast as her naughty little legs could carry her, all the way out of the theatre doors and along the gravel path at the front of the school. She glanced behind her to see if the creature was chasing her when – **TWHACK!**

Her foot caught the edge of something poking out of a bush and she went tumbling on to her bottom.

A large shadow fell over her, and Gemolina blinked her eyes open to find the Christmasaurus glaring down at her.

'PLEASE DON'T EAT ME!

I'M TOO TALENTED TO DIE!'

she cried dramatically.

The Christmasaurus let out a roar of laughter, and, even though Gemolina had never heard a dinosaur laugh before, she somehow knew that was what this creature was doing.

'So, you won't eat me?'

The Christmasaurus shook his head.

'But . . .

    you're . . .

        you're . . .

            you're a . . .

DINOSAUR!'

The Christmasaurus nodded.

'What are you doing at my school?'

The Christmasaurus carefully stuck his snout into the bush and dragged out the thing that had tripped Gemolina up. He did his best to ignore the twang of his wobbly tooth as he pulled out the heavy book – his toothache was getting worse and he shuddered at the thought of another visit from Gumdrop, but right now his secret mission to save Christmas was all that mattered! Gemolina brushed off the loose twigs and leaves and read the glistening words on the cover of the heavy black book.

'*The Naughty List,*' she whispered, letting it sink in. 'Whoa! You mean, *this* is Santa's actual Naughty List?'

The Christmasaurus nodded.

'Awesome!' She grinned, but the book suddenly burst open and began flicking through its pages until –

BAM!

A beam of light shone out on Gemolina's face from the words written within.

GEMOLINA SHINE

'I'm on the Naughty List?' she said in total shock. 'I always wanted my name in lights, but not like this! There has to be some mistake! I've not done anything –'

Before she could say the word *wrong*, the Christmasaurus blew a big fat raspberry in her face and stopped her from making any ridiculous excuses. He'd seen first-hand what she had been up to, wrecking poor Dorothy's audition.

By now he was good at getting to the heart of all these Naughty Listers, so he looked deep into her eyes, trying to let her know that he could *see* her. He could see the naughty actions and the mistakes but, more importantly, he could see the good hiding beneath them: the nice behind the naughty, just waiting for a second chance.

'Why are you looking at me like that?' Gemolina asked. 'Do you need the toilet? Because I'm pretty sure it's OK for you to just go in the bush.'

The Christmasaurus shook his head. OK, so perhaps his intense, meaningful stare wasn't quite perfected yet. He was going to have to find another way to show Gemolina what a naughty nincompoop she'd been.

There was a sudden commotion in the distance as a group of students gathered around the school noticeboard.

This was what Gemolina had been waiting for – the announcement of the Christmas soloist!

Immediately forgetting about the strange new dinosaur in her life, Gemolina rushed over to take a look at the noticeboard.

'Surprise, surprise. Gemolina got it. **AGAIN!**' she heard Levi Johnson scoff as she drew closer.

'She would have totally lost it if Dorothy had got the solo!' added Aleena George.

'Yeah, I heard Gemolina even tried poisoning Dorothy to try to stop her from auditioning,' whispered Levi.

'Well, we all know it was her who let all the school pets out –' said Aleena, laughing.

'I got that solo fair and square!' snapped Gemolina from behind them.

The pair spun round and the Christmasaurus leapt into the nearest tree before the children spotted him!

Levi gulped. 'Oh, hi, Gemolina . . . We didn't know you were there.'

'Yeah, well, I heard what you said and you're just jealous because *you* don't have what it takes to be a soloist like **ME**. Why don't you run along to choir practice and rehearse your **GROUP** song? Oh, wait, there's no point – no one will hear you anyway,' Gemolina cackled as she marched away.

Once Gemolina was on her own, the Christmasaurus caught up with her.

'You again? What do you want now?' she snapped.

The Christmasaurus was starting to realize this might just be his toughest case yet, and it was going to require some serious thinking, which wasn't easy for a dinosaur whose brain should have gone extinct millions of years ago! He needed to concentrate and come up with a plan. If only the sound of someone singing a beautiful carol wasn't quite so distracting . . .

Singing?

Wait a second – where was that voice coming from? He looked at Gemolina, whose ears had pricked up too at the musical sound.

As though they were reading each other's minds, Gemolina and the Christmasaurus followed the whisperings of the sad but beautiful song that was drifting on the wind and, before long, they found themselves at an open window outside the sports hall.

'That's the most beautiful voice I've ever heard!'

whispered Gemolina, who was a little bit in awe and a little bit worried that someone might actually be a better singer than her! The Christmasaurus had to agree – it was hauntingly beautiful, the kind of voice that should belong to a mermaid in a deserted lagoon.

'Who is it coming from?' asked Gemolina.

The Christmasaurus and Gemolina stretched up on their tippy-toes to peep inside. But the singing stopped instantly, and Gemolina caught sight of a figure in the middle of the room that quickly dashed out of the door.

Gemolina stumbled away from the window, looking like she'd seen a ghost.

'That beautiful voice. I think it belonged to Dorothy Dorkins!' she whispered in shock. 'Could it be true?' she asked the Christmasaurus.

There was only
ONE WAY to find out.

CHAPTER THIRTY-TWO
DOROTHY DORKINS

That evening after school, the Christmasaurus and Gemolina paid a visit to Dorothy Dorkins' house. It was easy to find because everyone knew that the Dorkins family lived IN THE SCHOOL!

Well, not exactly *in* the school. The family owned the house right next to the school gates, at the end of the playground. The small house had been there long before the school, and gradually the school had built up around it, meaning it sat just inside the grounds and every pupil had to walk past it in the morning. It had been there for so long that no one seemed to even notice

it any more. It was just sort of *there* but no one saw it.

A little bit like Dorothy.

You see, while Gemolina Shine was the beaming star at the centre of her world, Dorothy Dorkins was the exact opposite.

Dorothy had seven brothers – that's right, SEVEN! Their names were Dave, Daniel, then triplets Derek, Dean and Dominick, followed by Dylan and then baby Dawson. Living with seven brothers meant that Dorothy's house was **FULL** and **LOUD** with the boys bashing and banging into each other, causing chaos and creating catastrophes everywhere they went.

So where did Dorothy fit into all that? Well, the problem was that she didn't really. Dorothy lived in a murky middle, greyish area of attention. It was the place where she never really got her own way, but also wasn't totally left out so that people felt bad enough to make a fuss of her. She was just sort of . . . invisible.

So invisible, in fact, that none of Dorothy's seven brothers even knew what Dorothy really loved doing more than anything else in the whole wide, ever-expanding universe.

Dorothy Dorkins loved to **SING!** Which is exactly why she had wanted to try out for the school solo. Each Christmas, she had watched as Gemolina took to the stage, shining brightly in the lights as her parents glowed with pride in the crowd. And, each Christmas, Dorothy had wished that she could have just one tiny moment in the spotlight, so that maybe she could make her parents glow with pride like that. This year she had plucked up all her courage and signed up to audition, even though deep down she hadn't thought she was anywhere near good enough to actually be chosen. And, with every setback and accident at each audition, a little bit of that confidence she'd found to perform had been taken away.

Now she was back home in the safety of her own house, able to sing and sing and sing without worrying about what anyone might be saying about silly, boring Dorothy Dorkins thinking she could possibly take on the big Christmas solo!

'Christmas lights are glowing,
There's magic everywhere . . .'

DOROTHY DORKINS

Dorothy's beautiful voice drifted from beyond the front door as Gemolina and the Christmasaurus approached. They didn't ring the doorbell but cheekily peered in through the window at the side of the doorway and saw Dorothy sitting on the stairs, singing to herself while her brothers raced up and down them.

'Outside it's started snowing,
There's winter in the air . . .'

'DOROTHY, can you hand me the baby wipes? Your brother has a REALLY stinky nappy!' shouted Dorothy's dad, and she stopped singing to help.

'Ew, that's SO gross!' Dorothy winced, pinching her nose as she hurried to the kitchen, and away from baby Dawson's explosive bottom, for a more pleasant place to sing.

She opened her mouth and was about to start singing again when . . .

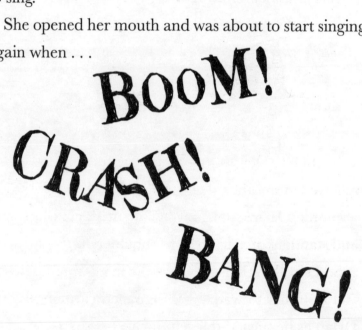

BOOM! CRASH! BANG!

Little Dominick started a deafening drum solo using the pots and pans in the kitchen, playing to a sold-out stadium of his favourite action figures.

Dorothy sighed and swiftly hid herself inside the small pantry. The acoustics were rubbish, but the packets of biscuits on the shelves helped block out some of her brother's noise!

'Every home is full of laughter,' she sang,
'And family talking all night long . . .'

BOOM!

In burst Derek searching for chocolate, closely followed by another of the triplets, Dean, as they plotted a cunning snack theft involving sticky tape, a spatula and standing on each other's shoulders.

So Dorothy tried singing in the living room, but . . .

'I'm trying to watch TV!' groaned cartoon-obsessed Dylan as he turned the volume up.

Upstairs, Daniel was shredding a mind-melting solo on his electric guitar (or at least pretending to while blasting rock music on his stereo).

Which left the top floor, where her sixteen-year-old brother Dave dwelt in a dark room that smelt of yesteryear's socks. She definitely didn't want to sing up there!

'Why isn't anyone listening to her sing?' Gemolina asked the Christmasaurus as they shuffled from one window to the next, watching Dorothy. 'In my house, when *I* sing, everybody stops to listen, no matter what they're doing!'

> *'But it doesn't feel like Christmas*
> *Without a Christmas song . . .'*

Dorothy perched back on her spot on the stairs and started singing softly to herself.

Gemolina suddenly felt a wave of sadness wash over her as she wondered what it must feel like to have music inside you that no one wants to hear.

'Oi, be quiet!' shouted Dylan.

'Yeah, I'm trying to play guitar!'
yelled Daniel.

'I just lost my game because of YOU!'
moaned Dave.

'You can sing if you give us chocolate!'
Derek and Dean said, grinning.

'Can't you sing at school or something?'
barked Dominick.

'I tried, but I wasn't
good enough to get the solo!'

Dorothy snapped and stormed off before they heard the
unmistakable sound of a bedroom door slamming.

The Christmasaurus looked at Gemolina and raised
his icy eyebrow.

'Don't look at me like that. I feel bad enough already!'
Gemolina confessed. The Christmasaurus gave a little

roar of excitement at his Naughty Lister feeling remorse.

'But it's too late now. My name is already down for the solo and my family are all coming to the show expecting me to sing. I can't let my fans down!' Gemolina said, trying to push down the guilty feeling rising in her chest.

The Christmasaurus walked Gemolina home in silence, trying to think of another way to change her mind.

'I'm sorry. I wish there was something I could do, but it's not *my* fault Mrs Symphony chose me to sing, is it?'

The Christmasaurus gave her a hard look.

'Anyway . . . I need to get an early night. Tomorrow is a big day!'

And, with that, Gemolina patted the Christmasaurus on his scaly head and went inside, leaving the dinosaur to wonder if Gemolina Shine might be destined to stay on the Naughty List for good.

Chapter Thirty-three
SHOWTIME

The school was electric with excitement as everyone made their final preparations for the big Christmas show.

There were shepherds coming and going from every classroom, trying to decide which style of fake beard made them look the shepherdiest; teachers were sticking what felt like thousands of cotton-wool balls on to sheep costumes; children dressed as donkeys were rehearsing their neighs; angels were flapping their tinfoil wings; and a rather concerned-looking Ishaan Dara from Reception was being hoisted above the stage dressed as a glittering, golden Christmas star, ready for his part at the end of the show.

As the parents started arriving, you could feel the nerves wash across the classrooms like a wave, all to the soundtrack of the school choir doing their last rehearsal in the distant music room.

Gemolina was in the star dressing room (the girls' toilets closest to the stage), doing some final practising in the mirror. She had sung the Christmas solo for the last five years running, but tonight, for the first time, she was nervous.

SHOWTIME

'**It's showtime!**' called Mrs Symphony, and the children began lining up, ready to take to the stage.

Once the audience had taken their seats, the Christmasaurus himself sneaked into the back of the theatre, where he found a cosy, hidden spot behind a Christmas tree that gave him a great view of the stage.

'Ladies and gentlemen, mums and dads, family and friends – welcome to our Christmas concert,' Mrs Symphony said as she appeared on stage from behind the curtain. 'The children have been working very hard on what I'm sure will be our best concert ever, featuring some wonderful group performances and the all-important Christmas solo that I know we've been waiting for. So, let the show begin!' And, with that, the curtain was raised and the Christmas show was underway.

There was laughter and cheers from the audience as they waved and cried at the children performing their highlights of the nativity story.

Then they were treated to a Christmas reading from Stephen Petry from Year

Four, during which at least five dads were spotted falling asleep, followed by a short dance from *The Nutcracker* by the kids from the nursery. Only two kids fell off the front of the stage (which was a big improvement on the previous year in which only one child was left standing by the end), then finally it was the choir.

Fifty children marched on to the stage, led by Gemolina Shine, who waved to the audience as they whooped and cheered. Dorothy Dorkins was there somewhere too, but finding her among the forty-nine other students was harder than finding Wally in the ancient copy of *Where's Wally?* you find in every dentist's waiting room (I'm sure they forgot to draw Wally in that one!). Even Dorothy's seven brothers, who were reluctantly watching in the audience with their parents, couldn't spot her.

'That's her at the back, isn't it?' said Derek.

'That's a boy!' corrected Dean.

'Well, it looks like Dorothy if you make your eyes go all blurry.'

The choir burst into a chirpy rendition of 'We Wish You a Merry Christmas', followed by a medley of

Christmas hits – all gearing up towards that final big moment in which Gemolina would bring the house down with her solo!

The choir finished.

The applause faded.

A single spotlight fell on a microphone placed centre stage.

This was it!

Gemolina stepped into the pool of light and the crowd cheered a little as the piano began to play. Gemolina took a deep breath and . . .

'**Stop!**' she said, holding up her hand.

There was a gasp from the crowd as the music was abruptly silenced, and Gemolina felt the hundreds of pairs of eyes in the audience watching her, wondering what was happening. Had she forgotten the words? Was she suffering from stage fright?

'I have sung the Christmas solo for five years.' There was a little *whoop* from the back of the audience. 'Thank you, Daddy! But, as I was saying, I have sung the solo for five years and the truth is, this year . . . I don't deserve it.'

The crowd gasped again.

'The Christmas solo is supposed to be the gift of song from our school, and there is someone else here who truly has the gift of song . . . and I think it's time to unwrap it!'

330

Showtime

The Christmasaurus couldn't help but release a little celebratory **roar** before having to duck behind the Christmas tree again. Gemolina was giving up her spotlight for someone else! Perhaps she would make it off the Naughty List, after all!

'So, this year, the Christmas solo will be sung by Dorothy Dorkins,' Gemolina announced.

There was a stunned silence from the audience as Dorothy Dorkins nervously stepped out from her position in the choir.

'Found her!' whispered her seven brothers.

Dorothy's footsteps echoed around the quiet theatre as she walked to the spotlight.

'*What are you doing?*' Dorothy whispered to Gemolina.

'I've had plenty of moments to shine – now it's your turn. I'm sorry – it was me who did all those awful things to interrupt your auditions, but your voice is wonderful, Dorothy, and you deserve to get the chance to share it and be heard.'

'Are you sure?' Dorothy whispered, and Gemolina nodded, stepping away from the microphone and walking out of the spotlight.

'Oh, and, Dorothy? Break a leg!' Gemolina added from the shadows as the piano started to play and Dorothy sang.

'Christmas lights are glowing,
There's magic everywhere.
Outside it's started snowing,
There's winter in the air.
Every home is full of laughter
And family talking all night long.
But it doesn't feel like Christmas
Without a Christmas song.'

Dorothy's voice warmed every frosty heart inside that theatre, filling them all with the wondrous joy of Christmas. From centre stage, in the glow of the spotlight, Dorothy caught sight of her seven brothers, whose mouths were wide open but no noise was coming

out for a change, and, next to them, the beaming smiles of her proud parents.

When she finished, there was an eruption of applause, laughter and tears of happiness as the Christmas lights were switched on, transforming the room into a glistening wonderland. Finally, little Ishaan, the Christmas star, was released from the ceiling, swinging like a shooting star across the stage, wishing everyone a merry Christmas!

After the concert, Dorothy stepped out of the school theatre to another round of applause from the parents waiting outside to meet their children, while Gemolina slipped away unnoticed but with a wonderful warm smile on her face.

'*Gemstone!*' cried Mrs Shine. 'What a wonderful thing you did.'

'We're proud of you, Gem-gem!' added Mr Shine.

Gemolina heard the bush by the side of the theatre give a little rustle.

'I'll meet you at the car – I just want to say goodbye to a friend,' Gemolina said, waving her parents away as she headed towards the shaking shrubbery. She peered inside and found her blue dinosaur friend wiping away tears of happiness from his icy eyes.

'Are you OK?' she asked, smiling.

The Christmasaurus nodded happily.

'Bet you thought I was going to keep that solo all for myself, didn't you?'

The Christmasaurus laughed and nodded.

'So, about that Naughty List . . .'

The Christmasaurus held the book out in his claws for Gemolina to see.

'No, it's OK – I don't want to see it. I don't mind if I'm still on the Naughty List. I used to think that being the star of the show was the best feeling in the world, but what I did tonight for Dorothy – that feeling is worth more than a million solos! I don't need a list to tell me that.'

SHOWTIME

The Christmasaurus tucked the Naughty List under his tiny arm, so full of pride that he felt like he might pop.

'Well, thanks for your help. If I did make it back to the Nice List, it's only because you showed me the way. Merry Christmas!' Gemolina smiled and gave the Christmasaurus a big, festive hug.

As she walked back to her parents' car, she heard a gust of wind *Swoosh* through the leaves behind her and when she turned back the Christmasaurus had vanished into the starlight on his way to the next name on the Naughty List.

CHAPTER THIRTY-FOUR

WHERE'S WILLIAM?

After leaving Gemolina, the Christmasaurus galloped across the sky, clutching the glowing Naughty List in his claws. Even though each Naughty-Lister-turned-nice had helped him get one step closer to completing his mission to restore the balance of Christmas, the icy blue dinosaur couldn't help but wish that the next stop would finally be to see his best friend, William Trundle. He still couldn't understand how his best friend in the whole world could possibly have done anything naughty enough to end up on the

wrong list!

With each day that passed, Christmas Eve drew closer, and the Christmasaurus was starting to worry about what might happen if he didn't make it to William in time!

But it seemed that William would have to wait a little longer, because the Naughty List wasn't done yet. Next up it led the dinosaur to Jackson Humphreys, another child who had stumbled on to the Naughty List and was in need of nudging back to the nice one.

After **Jackson**

it was **Kajal Joshi,**

followed by **Maya Stewart,**

then **another**

and **another**

and **another**

337

until eventually the Christmasaurus had spent almost all December soaring around the globe, following the light to the children most in need of second chances. Now there were just **TWO DAYS** until Christmas! Time to help William was running out, but with each Naughty Lister came a new challenge to overcome. Like Jason Perry, the non-believer who thought Santa was a conspiracy invented by the government to get kids to go to bed early.

Obviously a flying dinosaur tumbling down his chimney helped open his mind to impossible things.

Then there was Buddy Fletcher, who was always taking his clothes off at school and running around totally nuddy. Buddy was getting into so much trouble for it, until the Christmasaurus discovered he was allergic to the material of his uniform! A new pair of hypoallergenic pants, socks and all the trimmings later and

HEY PRESTO!

No more uncomfortable itching for Buddy, and no more wild bums in the playground.

The Christmasaurus cured a regular nose-picker of their horrible habit; showed a wall-scribbler how to focus their artistic talent on paper, NOT the walls; and reminded at least three pairs of bickering siblings that it takes far more effort to be mean to someone than it does to be polite.

Each visit made the Naughty List feel lighter as more and more names were relocated to the Nice List. As he travelled, the Christmasaurus could almost picture Santa's weighing scales adjusting, bringing the balance back towards being level. In fact, now the Naughty List was barely glowing at all, as child after child put right their wrongs with the help of the Christmasaurus. And so, with just days until Christmas Eve, there was finally just enough light left to lead our dinosaur friend to one last child on the Naughty List . . .

CHAPTER THIRTY-FIVE
WILLIAM TRUNDLE

One Week Earlier –
SEVEN DAYS UNTIL CHRISTMAS EVE!

William Trundle loved dinosaurs, which was good because his best friend happened to be one. That's right – William and the Christmasaurus had been the best of friends ever since they shared a wild adventure one Christmas Eve trying to escape an evil hunter who wanted the poor Christmasaurus's head on his wall. **Yuck!**

After that, they had another adventure travelling across frozen time and space to save the future of Christmas itself. So let's just say the two friends had been through **A LOT** together and, even though they only got to see each other once a year, they both knew that a friend is for life, not just for Christmas.

When it comes to nice kids, the Christmasaurus was sure there was no one nicer than William. He was top of the pile! So how on earth had he come to be on the Naughty List?

Let's find out . . .

❄

'Brenda and I are hitting the shops today. Fancy tagging along, Willypoos?' asked Pamela, William's stepmum, as she served up the traditional Saturday morning pancakes.

'Actually, Dad, can I come to work with you today?' William pleaded with his dad.

'Sure!' Bob Trundle grinned. He loved that his son took an interest in his work.

'The museum again?' said William's stepsister, Brenda, letting out a snort. 'You've been there hundreds of times, William! Don't you find it boring?'

'Boring? A building filled with thousands of ancient fossils of incredible creatures that walked the Earth millions of years ago? **NO WAY!**' William said cheerily as he took a bite of his syrup-drenched pancake.

'You two are such nerds,' Brenda teased.

'I can't argue with that!' Bob smiled, giving his son a high-five.

'Plus, I want to pick up the latest copy of *Fossil Hunter* magazine from the gift shop. It's got all the latest discoveries from Dino Cove,' said William.

'Dino-*what*?' Brenda scoffed through a mouthful of fluffy pancake.

'Dino Cove. It's a sweet spot on the Jurassic coast in Dorset, where literally thousands of new dinosaur fossils are discovered each year,' William explained.

'That's right. In fact, we have a new fossil at the museum that was just discovered at Dino Cove,' Bob added.

'Really?' William's ears perked up with excitement.

'Yeah, the archaeologists know it's a tooth, but it's a bit of a mystery as they can't work out which dinosaur it belonged to!'

William shovelled the rest of his pancakes into his mouth so fast he barely tasted them.

'Right, I'm ready! Can we go?' William panted, and a few minutes later they were in the car on their way.

Bob had worked at the museum for many years. He'd started off selling ice creams at the cafe, then had been promoted to stacking the souvenirs at the gift shop. Slowly he'd worked his way up, and now he managed the whole shop! The gift shop was Bob's pride and joy. He loved working in a place where kids could find a little bit of history to take home with them.

More recently, though, Bob had branched out of the gift shop and started working part-time as a TOUR GUIDE.

He was AMAZING at it!

No one knew the museum better than Bob Trundle, plus, when it came to telling stories, he was the master.

He had one of those voices that made anything sound interesting, and somehow he could make even the most snoringly boring fossils come alive with magic.

The only thing Bob didn't like about working at the museum was his new boss, Mrs Brutelle, who had recently been appointed as the Museum Governor. Here she is and, as you can see, she was quite an intimidating person to have towering over your every move!

Mrs Brutelle was as stern as they come, and for some reason she didn't seem to like Bob very much. Perhaps it had something to do with the time he accidentally ordered five hundred Christmas trees for the gift shop Christmas display, which pushed the museum over their budget (although everyone thought it looked spectacular).

But having a boss who didn't like him only made Bob want to work harder to prove her wrong, and he always wanted every tour to be more magical than the last.

'Over here we have a special fossil known as *coprolite*!' Bob announced that morning as he gathered a group of children around a large lumpy fossil. William crowded round with them, tagging along on the tour. He hoped that the new dinosaur tooth would be coming up soon!

'We want to see killer teeth and deadly claws, not stupid old rocks!' moaned one boy, stretching over the barrier and snatching the fossil out of its display stand.

'Stephen, put that back!' snapped the boy's mum.

Bob just smiled. 'It's OK. Have a look at it, Stephen. Give it a real close inspection and see if you can tell me what that *stupid old rock* is that you're touching.'

'Dunno.' The boy shrugged, turning the ancient rock in his hands.

'Well, why don't you give it a good rub and see if you can feel anything on the surface?' Bob grinned and gave William a wink as Stephen started rubbing the rock with his palm.

'Good. Now give it a sniff – does it *smell* of anything?' Bob asked, and the boy held it to his nose and gave it a deep sniff before shaking his head.

'Just smells like a boring rock.'

'That's strange, it must have lost its smell,' Bob said.

'Lost its smell? Don't be ridiculous. Rocks. Don't. Smell,' scoffed Stephen.

'Well, *rocks* don't, but you're not holding a rock. You're holding a lump of

fossilized dinosaur POO!'

Bob revealed, and the group of children erupted into fits of laughter, trying to leap away from the ancient dino-poop as Stephen went bright red and quickly flung it on the floor before running away.

'Right, on with the tour!' Bob announced, leading the group into the next exhibit hall. 'Willypoos, put the poo back in the display, would you?'

'OK, Dad, I'll catch you up!' William replied.

Just before his dad shepherded the tour into the next room, he turned back and said, 'Oh, and, William, *that's* the tooth I was telling you about from Dino Cove!'

William followed his gaze to a tall plinth just in front of him, on the other side of the security rope. On top sat a magnificent fossilized dinosaur tooth, gleaming in spotlights like the Crown Jewels. It was curved like a crescent moon and still looked sharp, even after being buried for millions of years.

'**Whoa!**' William whispered, as he read the little plaque that said:

THE MYSTERIOUS TOOTH OF DINO COVE
DINOSAUR TOOTH
SPECIES: UNKNOWN
DISCOVERED: DINO COVE, JURASSIC COAST

William started imagining what it must have felt like to have found that fossil lying among the pebbles on the beach. He wished more than anything that he could go there one day.

He bent down and scooped up the coprolite fossil from the floor and rolled it over in his hands with a chuckle. He glanced around the empty hall to make sure no one was looking, then couldn't resist giving the rock a sniff.

Nope, no smell. Millions of years is definitely long enough to get rid of **poo pong!**

William reached over the security rope to place the

coprolite back on its display stand, but, as he did so, William couldn't help but notice that his hand was just a few inches away from the fossilized tooth!

If he wanted to, he could simply touch it, just gently. No one would know . . .

He knew he shouldn't. He knew he *mustn't*. He knew he would be in SO much trouble if he got caught . . .

So William DIDN'T do it.

Of course he didn't! This is *William Trundle* we're talking about! The nicest kid around, remember? But we all know he did *something* to get on that Naughty List, so what was it?

After replacing the fossilized faeces, William spun his chair round to catch up with his dad's tour, and *that's* when it happened.

As he turned, the push-handle of his wheelchair stuck out just far enough over the security rope to nudge the plinth holding the mysterious tooth! It wasn't hard. It only clipped it the tiniest bit – BUT it was enough to make the whole plinth . . .

wobble . . .

WOBBLE . . .

WOBBLE!

William glanced over his shoulder to see the tooth's plinth lean dramatically one way, then tilt the other, like some strange game of Fossil Jenga that was about to fall at any moment!

'No, no, no!' William whispered as he watched helplessly. 'Please don't fall over! Please!'

And, as though the fossil gods were listening, the plinth stopped wobbling. Just like that! William let out a big sigh of relief.

Are you waiting for a **BUT?**

OK, here it comes.

BUT the second that William thought it was all over, the tooth – which had come loose from all the wobbling

– slipped right off its display stand and went tumbling down to the cold, hard museum floor.

William watched it fall in what felt like slow motion, absolutely powerless to stop what happened next. The irreplaceable tooth hit the concrete and CRACKED in half.

UH-OH! I'm in BIG trouble,

he thought, but things were about to get a whole lot worse for William.

CHAPTER THIRTY-SIX

IT GETS WORSE
FOR WILLIAM

Now, we all know what William *should* have done next, don't we? That's right: find his dad and explain what had happened. If anyone would understand, it was Bob! It was an accident, these things happen. OK, so most of the time accidents don't involve destroying irreplaceable fossils worth thousands of pounds, but still William's dad would know that there are more important things than dead dinosaur bones.

'Nothing is more important than dead dinosaur bones . . .' Bob's voice boomed to his tour group in the next hall.

William's heart was beating so hard in his chest that he could see it bouncing around under his T-shirt.

What do I do? What do I do?

he thought to himself, staring at the two halves of the tooth.

Maybe I can fix it?
I could put it back together, like a puzzle.

And that was when it happened – when William made the decision that would lead to his name making its way on to the Naughty List. Instead of telling his dad what happened, William secretly scooped up the two halves of the tooth and slipped them into his pocket!

I know, right! What a wally! In fact, maybe we should change his name to WALLYam just for that.

If you're thinking, *That was a terrible decision that will go horribly wrong and come back to bite him on the bottom,* then you win ten points (but don't get too excited – points don't really mean anything . . . they're pointless points).

As William put the tooth in his pocket, Mrs

Brutelle marched into the room on one of her regular inspection rounds, so he was stuck. He knew straight away he'd made a terrible mistake, but there was no way of putting it back without being spotted. So William kept the cracked tooth in his pocket and caught up with his dad's tour in the next room. The fossil in his pocket felt so heavy and bulky that surely everyone could see it, and William broke into a guilty sweat as he became acutely aware of hundreds of pairs of eyes around the museum hall. Was it just in his imagination, or was everyone looking at him? He felt like everyone knew his secret, and the whole room started spinning around him.

Calm down, William, he told himself. *It'll all be OK. Just get home, fix the tooth and then put it back!*

NO ONE saw a thing!
NO ONE will ever know!

DING-A-LING-A-LING-A-LING-A-LING-A-LING-A-LING-A-LING!

A piercing alarm screeched through the halls of the museum, stopping everyone in their tracks.

'Emergency! Emergency!'

boomed two burly security guards into their walkie-talkies as they bounded through the exhibits. 'A fossil has been STOLEN!'

'Oh no!' Bob cried. 'The tour's over, I'm afraid, kids. There's a fossil thief on the loose. William, could you . . . William? WILLIAM?'

But William wasn't there any more.

The moment he saw the security guards, William panicked and made a dash for the door, skidding through the museum, weaving in and out of flustered tourists until he was out in the freedom of the cool morning air. He didn't stop until he was home, where he wheeled straight to his room, closed the door and emptied the *accidentally* stolen contents of his pocket on to his homework desk.

'Oh no!' William gasped. The two halves of the tooth had somehow cracked into FIVE smaller pieces.

'It must have been crushed in my pocket!' William

cried. He reached out to touch the fragments, but, as he did, the ancient, fossilized tooth cracked again, this time into nothing more than crumbs!

'Willypoos, are you home?' Bob called from the hallway as he burst in the front door.

William quickly opened his top drawer and scooped all the pieces of dinosaur tooth inside and hid them under his pants and socks, just as his dad rushed into his bedroom.

'There you are! I didn't know where you'd gone. I was worried sick,' Bob said, giving William a big, relieved hug. 'You can't leave like that without telling me!'

'Sorry, Dad,' William said nervously. He knew now was the time to confess and hope his dad would understand. 'Listen, about that missing tooth –'

'It's awful! The whole museum is being turned upside down right now.' Bob sighed, clearly very stressed about the whole thing.

'Oh. Well, the thing is –'

'Whoever stole that tooth is going to be in big trouble!' Bob interrupted. **'BIG trouble!'**

'Really?' William gulped.

'Oh yes! Prison, probably. I mean, you can't just go around taking priceless fossils!'

William suddenly changed his mind about telling his dad that the missing dinosaur tooth was actually sitting in the drawer with his underwear!

DING-DONG!

The doorbell rang.

'Who on earth could that be?' Bob said.

DING-DONG!
DING-DONG!
DING-DONG!

'All right! I'm coming!' Bob muttered when the doorbell didn't stop ding-donging.

He opened the door to a sudden explosion of bright flashes and discovered a dozen journalists and photographers waiting on the doorstep of their wonky house.

IT GETS WORSE FOR WILLIAM

'Is it true there's a fossil thief at large in the area?' one of the journalists called.

'Did you see anyone suspicious in the museum?' added another.

'Could the other fossils be at risk?' threw in another reporter. None of them actually gave Bob a moment to answer any of their questions, even if he'd wanted to!

'Robert Trundle, we've been informed that you were the last museum official to be in the room before the fossil was stolen. Are you going to resign if the tooth isn't found?'

William, who was spying from the doorway of his bedroom, felt a knot twist in his stomach at those words. Surely his dad wouldn't really lose his job because of this? Bob loved working at the museum; he couldn't let that happen. But if Bob was right and William confessed that he was the thief, would he go to prison?!

William wasn't sure what was worse!

'**No c-c-comment!**' Bob spluttered anxiously as he closed the door. William followed him into the living room.

'Dad, are you OK?'

'Not right now, Willypoos. I've got to make some phone calls. Why don't you watch some cartoons or something,' Bob said in a daze, switching the TV on for William before picking up the phone.

'*BREAKING NEWS!*' blasted the TV as the presenter stared intensely down the lens. '*In the last hour, a priceless dinosaur tooth has been reported STOLEN from the Whiffington Museum. The thief is on the run and now armed with a very pointy, although very old, object.*'

Bob and William stood gawping at the TV as their wonky little house suddenly appeared on the screen.

'Dad, our house is on the telly!' William gawked.

'Our reporter tried to get an update from Robert Trundle, the last member of the museum staff to see the tooth, but Mr Trundle refused to comment.'

Bob's worried face popped up on the TV screen, looking all nervous and flustered.

'No c-c-comment,' he said.

'Dad, now you're on the TV,' William whispered.

'Yeah,' replied Bob in total shock.

'The museum has released a statement pleading for the safe return of the mysterious, unidentified dinosaur tooth, which was set to become a big attraction for museum visitors. Could this missing tooth be the root of more trouble for the museum? One thing is for sure: no fossil is safe until this fugitive is found.'

The special report ended, and Bob switched the TV off.

'I'm . . . famous,' Bob said.

I'm a FUGITIVE, William thought.

'Come on,' Bob said, grabbing his coat and car keys.

'Where are we going?' William asked, racing down the hallway after his dad, who suddenly flung the front door open and declared to the world:

'I, Bob Trundle, am going to find that thief!'

But the journalists and photographers had gone and had been replaced by the unmistakably intimidating figure of Mrs Brutelle, Bob's boss, who was making her way towards the house!

'Very good, Mr Trundle. And I should think so too, since *you* were the last museum employee to see the fossil. I will hold *you* personally responsible if it is not back on its plinth in one week from today!' she hissed.

'One week? But that's Christmas Eve!'

'And?' snapped Mrs Brutelle.

'And . . . it's the last day at work before Christmas,' Bob said in a small voice.

'Yes, and if you don't find it by then, it will be your last day full stop. You will never set foot inside *my* museum again. Good luck.' And, with that, she spun on the heels of her boots and marched away.

Bob closed the front door and rested his head on it for a moment, thinking.

'If I were a fossil thief, where would I be?' he muttered to himself, and William couldn't help but imagine that if they were in a panto this would be the moment when all the audience would scream

'He's behind you!'

as his dad was totally unaware that the fossil thief was his own son, sitting barely a few feet away, wishing for a way out of this disaster.

Well maybe, just maybe, William's wish was about to come true.

CHAPTER THIRTY-SEVEN

WILLIAM AND THE CHRISTMASAURUS

ONE DAY UNTIL CHRISTMAS EVE!

THUMP!

William woke up with a start. His dad had slammed a big pile of paperwork at the foot of his bed.

'Wakey-wakey, Watson!' Bob chirped.

'Wats-who?' William croaked as he rubbed his eyes

to see his dad clutching a magnifying glass in one hand and a torch in the other as he began to study the sheets of paper in front of him.

'It's too early, Dad!' William moaned, noticing that the sun hadn't even risen yet.

'Yes, and the early bird catches the fossil thief,' Bob said, grinning.

It's fair to say that Bob had taken the task of discovering the true identity of the fossil thief and uncovering its location VERY seriously. For the last few days he had woken William at the crack of dawn, but instead of delivering warm vaninnamon pancakes (vanilla + cinnamon = vaninnamon!) like he usually did in December, he delivered the local newspaper and a pen for William so they could search for new clues. This wasn't just his job at stake; this was about rescuing the poor fossil and 'restoring justice' (as Bob put it).

'Don't you think you should leave catching criminals to the police?' Pamela asked over the breakfast table, though it was scattered with so many photos of dinosaur teeth and museum maps that you couldn't actually see any breakfast.

'Nonsense. What do the police know about rare fossils? This case requires a specialist,' Bob said proudly as he dashed out of the door like super-spy Zack Danger.

'Your dad has seen one too many Indiana Jones films.' said Brenda, laughing.

William couldn't help but agree that his dad almost seemed to be enjoying this new role as a fossil-hunting vigilante. The local newspaper even ran a story about Bob, calling him

SHERLOCK BONES,

which he had framed and hung in the bathroom.

In fact, Bob had become so obsessed with 'cracking this case' that he'd forgotten some of his regular Christmas traditions! Instead of wearing his musical, light-up Christmas jumpers each day, he'd switched to black knitted sweaters that he said helped him 'blend in' to his surroundings while searching for the fossil thief. Instead of watching the Christmas Movie Channel, he insisted they had the twenty-four hour news channel on TWENTY-FOUR HOURS a day! Even the Christmas playlist on car journeys had been switched for podcasts about criminal-tracking techniques!

For the first time in William's life, Bob Trundle – aka the most Christmassy man alive – wasn't very Christmassy!

AND IT WAS ALL WILLIAM'S FAULT!

While Pamela and Brenda decorated the living room with the fairy lights that Bob had been too busy to hang, Bob used the time to study technical maps of the museum, noting every possible escape route the tooth-thief might have taken. Then the next day he and William retraced them in search of clues.

Of course, William knew that all this was totally useless as *he* was the one they were looking for, but it had gone too far now. There was no going back. With each passing day, telling his dad the truth seemed more and more impossible.

The week had flown by faster than a blue dinosaur, and William's chances of successfully repairing the fossil were looking slimmer and slimmer. Each night, after the 'fossil-thief-hunting' was finished for the day, William had been trying to put the broken tooth back together, but he wasn't having much luck and it was now the twenty-third of December, the day before Christmas Eve (or Christmas Eve Eve as Bob Trundle usually called it when he wasn't so wrapped up in solving crimes and saving his job!). But it was understandable that Bob wasn't feeling his usual merry self as the week was almost over, and if that tooth wasn't back on the display by tomorrow morning when the museum opened then William's dad was done for!

When Pamela placed the dinner plates on the table, not even her attempt to cheer up her husband with an early Christmas dinner could distract him from his mission. The food stayed untouched on his plate as he slipped on his jacket to head out into the night.

'Where are you going?' Pamela asked.

'I'm going to camp out at the museum. Tonight is my last chance to catch that crook!' Bob said hopefully.

'I really don't think your thief is just going to show up at the scene of the crime again,' said Brenda, but Bob was already running into the darkness like Batman – well, except he was wearing a black knitted sweater instead of baddie-proof armour, and drove a rusty yellow people-carrier instead of a Batmobile, but, suit or no suit, Bob the vigilante and the *Bobmobile* were gone.

Pamela sighed. 'I really hope he finds that tooth.'

'Not a chance,' Brenda said. 'It's already been a week. That thief will be **LONG** gone by now. Probably sold the tooth for a suitcase full of cash, left the country and gone on the run!'

'No, they haven't,' William snapped.

'How do you know? Was it *you* who stole it?' Brenda fired back.

The kitchen fell silent.

William didn't breathe.

How did she know?

How long had she known?

What would happen now?

'PAH-HA-HA!'

Brenda cackled. 'You should see your face! As if perfect William Trundle would ever steal anything!'

❄

When William got to his room that night, he opened his drawer and pulled out the tooth fragments and a glue gun. Even though he'd been piecing it back together for a week now, it didn't look like a dinosaur tooth yet. More like a lump of gluey mud with bits of broken rock jutting out of it, but, just like his dad, William wasn't giving up. He had one night left! So, while his dad was out stalking shadows around the museum, William worked by torchlight and tried his hardest to piece the tooth back together.

The tense hours ticked by, and William kept gluing and holding and sticking and puzzling over the misshapen fossil. The time on his bedside clock kept getting later, and, without realizing it, William had fallen asleep.

THUD!

William was startled awake.

'Dad, it's too early,' he grumbled instinctively, but his dad didn't reply. **THUMP!**

371

He sat up, realizing that he'd fallen asleep at his desk. There was no one else in the room with him.

THUD! THUMP!

This time he heard the sound properly, and it was coming from the roof! For a moment he thought it might be Santa, but it was only Christmas Eve Eve – there was still one day to go before Santa would be stomping around on the roof, so it couldn't be him.

THUD! THUMP! BANG!

This time the noises sounded like they came from INSIDE the house.

William grabbed his torch and headed down the hall to the living room.

'Brenda?' he whispered as he peered into the room. 'Dad? PamelaaaAAAAAH!' He let out a squeal of fright as a cloud of black soot suddenly puffed out of the chimney, followed by a filthy dinosaur.

'CHRISTMASAURUS!' William cheered at seeing his best friend arrive in his fireplace.

The Christmasaurus fell into the room and instantly leapt on to William, licking his face like an excited puppy.

'OK! OK! I'm happy to see you too!' William laughed.

The Christmasaurus rolled around the room with a dino-sized grin on his face. It had been a long journey and he was finally with his friend! He felt just as at home here in the Trundles' cosy living room as he did in the grand halls of Santa's Snow Ranch.

'You must be hungry! Come on – let's see what snacks we've got in the kitchen,' whispered William.

A few minutes later, the two of them were on the kitchen floor eating mince pies by torchlight, laughing and giggling like they'd never been apart.

THE CHRISTMASAURUS AND THE NAUGHTY LIST

Three whole packets of mince pies and four pints of milk later, William was full and the Christmasaurus's wobbly tooth was aching, so they slumped back with full tummies and big smiles. William had even managed to forget about the fact that he was a wanted criminal for a few happy moments.

'I'm really glad to see you, but what are you doing here, Chrissy?' William asked. 'Shouldn't you be helping Santa get ready for the big day?'

A stern look suddenly fell on the Christmasaurus's face.

'What is it?' William asked.

The Christmasaurus marched back to the fireplace, stuck his snout into the chimney flue and when he came out he was carrying the heavy black book.

'Oh . . . I remember that,' William said. He'd seen the Naughty and Nice Lists the year before when he had visited the North Pole.

'Why have you got the Naughty List?' he asked, nervously backing away from the great tome as the Christmasaurus set it down on the kitchen table.

The list magically burst open to reveal a page with

two glowing words that illuminated William's face:

WILLIAM TRUNDLE!

He couldn't look the Christmasaurus in the eye.

'I thought this might happen.' He sniffled as a tear formed in the corner of his eye.

The Christmasaurus closed the book with his nose and nuzzled into William's shoulder. Naughty List or not, nothing would ever stop them being best friends.

The Christmasaurus grunted a little determined roar and gave William a nudge.

'You want to help?' asked William.

The Christmasaurus nodded so hard his icy mane jingled like a glass windchime caught in a breeze.

'OK, OK!' William smiled. 'Follow me . . .'

CHAPTER THIRTY-EIGHT
A BLUE HOPE

'*T*his is why I'm on the Naughty List.' He sighed, opening his drawer and pulling out the misshapen, badly repaired, fossilized dinosaur tooth.

The Christmasaurus screwed up his face –

GROSS!

'I know. It was an accident. I was in the museum, and my wheelchair knocked it, and it just fell and broke! I didn't steal it! Or, at least, I didn't *mean* to. I panicked, and then I thought I could fix it and return it without anyone noticing. But, well, look at it!' William held up the thing that was once a tooth. A little lump of rock fell to the floor. It now looked like a bit of plasticine that someone had rolled around in gravel.

'Now I've only got until tomorrow to fix it and put it back in the museum, otherwise my dad is going to be fired! Do you think you can help me, Chrissy?' William said, not feeling overly confident that the clumsy claws of the Christmasaurus were what this fossil needed.

His dinosaur friend leant in close to examine the tiny bits of fossil tooth. Dust made its way up his nostrils . . . tickling the back of his nose . . . the bit that made it impossible not to . . .

ACHOO!

The Christmasaurus sneezed what was left of the terribly repaired tooth into oblivion!

Puff! It was gone!

There was nothing left but dust and crumbs. The Christmasaurus looked at William with an expression that could only be translated as OOOPS!

'Well, now it's totally hopeless!' William said, dropping his head on his desk in defeat.

BUMP!

The bump caused something on his desk to fall over, landing on William's head. It was his copy of *Fossil Hunter* magazine from the museum gift shop.

'WAIT! THAT'S IT!'

William gasped, waving the magazine in the air as an idea bounced around his brain. 'We don't have to repair this tooth. We can REPLACE it with another one!'

He opened the magazine to a fold-out map of Dino Cove and held his torch steady for the Christmasaurus to see.

'This is where that tooth was discovered, which means there MUST be more teeth on that beach too!' William looked at the clock. It was 2 a.m.! He turned to the Christmasaurus. 'You're used to flying around the world and doing the impossible in one night, right, Chrissy? Fancy a late-night trip to the Jurassic Coast?'

The Christmasaurus nodded excitedly, already hopping on the spot, ready for an adventure.

'I've had too many winter adventures in my PJs!' William laughed as he threw on a warm jacket and a hat. Then, quickly and quietly, they made their way back down the hall, through the kitchen (where William stuffed the last two mince pies in his pocket for later) and then out into the frosty garden, where William unrolled the hosepipe and looped it around the Christmasaurus as reins.

'So, we fly to Dino Cove, find ourselves a tooth and get it back to the museum before it opens so we can save my dad's job!' William said, and the Christmasaurus roared in agreement.

William took a breath and couldn't suppress the smile that spread across his face at the realization that he was about to do his most favourite thing in the whole world.

'FLY, Christmasaurus! FLY!'

he called, and the Christmasaurus galloped across the lawn, pulling William behind like Santa's sleigh as he leapt into the air, skimming the neighbour's greenhouse, and soared into the sky, heading towards Dino Cove.

Had any of the children tucked in their beds below looked out of their windows, they would have seen nothing more than a shooting star streak across the black sky in a flash of blue. Then, before William had even a chance to take in the beautiful sight of the fields passing by beneath his wheels, the Christmasaurus used his new-found sense of speed and they were descending towards the Jurassic Coast.

'That's it!'

William shouted, pointing to a moonlit beach with an unmissable cliff formation – three towering rocks that rose from the black water, like the horns of a gigantic triceratops that could be resting beneath the waves.

The Christmasaurus made a perfect landing and William's wheels touched down with a gentle hiss on the slightly frozen sand, scattering loose pebbles as he pulled the brakes.

'I can't believe we're actually here!' William beamed, holding up the map from his magazine and looking around at the empty beach.

'OK, Christmasaurus – let's get digging!'

CHAPTER THIRTY-NINE
ANOTHER TOOTH

'The magazine says that the best place to start is over there, by that cave,' William said, pointing to a dark hole in the cliffs that lined the back of the beach. 'The fossils are inside the rock structures and cliffs, then, as they're beaten by the water and wind, the rocks break apart and erode, releasing new fossils all the time!'

The Christmasaurus pulled William across the beach, towards the enormous cave at the back.

'Now all we have to do is look,' William said, clicking his torch on and shining it on to the ground before leaning over the armrest of his wheelchair to get as close a look as possible at the rocks around him.

The Christmasaurus crouched so low that his nose was touching the cold rocks, sniffing them one by one in search of a tooth.

After about ten minutes, the Christmasaurus turned to William and gave a little chirp.

'Nope, nothing. Have you seen anything?'

The Christmasaurus shook his head.

The beach might have been famous for fossils, but most people who came looking for them came in the daylight – not in the middle of the night with nothing but a torch!

'It's so hard to see!' William complained. 'We need more light.'

His torch was bright, but on the vast shoreline it was only able to light up a tiny piece of the beach at a time. Then, suddenly, as William waved his torch over the glistening stones and pebbles all around them, the light caught the Christmasaurus's translucent, icy mane. The torchlight instantly split into hundreds of blue beams, illuminating their entire surroundings.

'Even if you weren't the only dinosaur on the planet, you'd still be the coolest!' William grinned, and they set to work, now with a beach as bright as a summer's day.

A few minutes later, the Christmasaurus let out an excited **ROAR!**

'What is it?' William said, pulling up next to his dino friend as the Christmasaurus carefully turned over a rock the size of William's fist.

There was a fossil inside it all right.

'Whoa, that's an ammonite!' William said, flicking through his magazine to the fossil index. 'It says here that they're related to squid and octopus! Good one! How incredible is it that we're the first to see that in millions of years?'

The Christmasaurus looked proud of himself for a second, but then remembered that they were on a mission – **a mission for a tooth!**

They both set back to work but after nearly an hour of searching they had only found a few plastic bottles (which William stuffed under his seat to recycle at home!), a dead crab and a rusty fishing hook.

'This is hopeless,' William said. 'It's freezing cold, and we've hardly scratched the surface of this beach.'

The Christmasaurus looked around at the huge stretch of beach ahead of them, and slumped to the pebbles with defeat. William was right. The chances of them finding a fossil to replace the broken tooth were next to none, which meant that Bob would be fired, William would remain on the Naughty List, the Christmasaurus would fail his secret mission to restore balance to the Naughty and Nice Lists, and Santa's future would still be at risk!

It was a lot to think about for a dinosaur.

William clicked off his torch and the two best friends sat for a moment staring out at the horizon, which already had a hint of the sunrise. It wouldn't be long before Mrs Brutelle would be opening up the doors to the museum. A museum that his dad would never be allowed in again.

The sad moment was interrupted by a strange gurgling sound that came from the Christmasaurus.

'Hungry?' William asked.

The Christmasaurus nodded.

'Here, have a mince pie,' William said, pulling out the snacks that he'd stashed in his pocket earlier.

The Christmasaurus was starving and opened his mouth for William to throw it in.

CRUNCH! CHOMP! YELP!

The Christmasaurus let out a painful roar.

'What's the matter?' William asked, seeing his friend wince as he rubbed his cheek.

The Christmasaurus opened his mouth to show William his wobbly tooth.

'Whoa, that looks ready to come out!'

There was silence for a moment as the two of them stared into each other's eyes, both having the same idea at the exact same time!

What was the one thing William needed?

A dinosaur tooth.

What was loose and ready to fall out of the Christmasaurus's mouth?

A DINOSAUR TOOTH!

'Christmasaurus – catch!' William grinned as he threw the last mince pie up into the air. The Christmasaurus instinctively opened his mouth to receive it.

CHOMP! CRUNCH! PING!

The wobbly tooth flew out of the Christmasaurus's mouth and landed with a

ANOTHER TOOTH

THUD on the sand at William's wheels.

William scooped it up and examined it closely, while the Christmasaurus enjoyed the rest of the treat with no pain!

'The tooth of a mysterious dinosaur, discovered at Dino Cove. This is PERFECT!' said William, brimming with joy. 'Now we just need to get it in the museum before Mrs Brutelle arrives!'

They took to the sky once more, racing towards the museum with the warmth of the morning sun on their backs. The beach below became fields, followed by villages that turned into towns and, before William could say **jingle all the way**, they were swooping down towards the grand exterior of the museum.

CHAPTER FORTY

SWITCHEROO

William and the Christmasaurus raced silently through the fossil displays as warm streaks of sunlight began beaming through the tall windows, casting long shadows of the skeletons that looked down on them.

'This way – hurry!' William hissed, his wheels squeaking on the polished floor as they rushed towards the room where William had broken the tooth. There, in the centre of it all, was an empty plinth with its dramatic spotlights only highlighting the fact that whatever usually rested on it was missing . . . **but not for long!**

SWITCHEROO

The two of them slowed as they approached, and William held out the Christmasaurus's tooth, ready to place it on top of the plinth.

'This is it!' William grinned. 'I can't believe we actually did it . . .'

He stretched his arm over the security rope and very carefully, inch by inch, centimetre by centimetre, millimetre by . . . well, you get the point! William carefully lowered the Christmasaurus's tooth on to the stand with a gentle **clink** as the enamel touched the cool metal.

'It's perfect,' William whispered with wide eyes, and the Christmasaurus stepped back, admiring his donation. One dinosaur tooth discovered at Dino Cove switched for *another* dinosaur tooth discovered at Dino Cove.

Now, if you're thinking that their adventure was over, and that William had saved the day, then you are totally **WRONG**, for William (and you!) had forgotten one thing. His dad, aka Sherlock Bones, was staking out the museum, hoping that the fossil thief would return . . .

'GOTCHA!'

Bob wailed as he sprung from the shadows, his black knitwear proving to be surprisingly effective camouflage. He knocked the Christmasaurus over and landed on top of him.

'I knew you'd return, you great big, fossil-stealing . . . dinosaur?'

'Dad! It's us!' William cried.

'W-W-William? Christmasaurus? What in the name of Christmas is going on?' Bob demanded, but, before William had a chance to explain anything, something caught Bob's eye.

'Hold on just a jingle. Is that . . . it *is*!

It's the TOOTH! YAHOO!'

Bob burst with joy, leaping around the room, spinning William and the Christmasaurus round in a circle as his cheers echoed around the hall.

'But, how did you find it? Did you catch the thief? Was it another one of your epic adventures? Tell me EVERYTHING!' Bob was smiling from ear to ear, desperate to hear the story of how his son had caught the infamous fossil thief and returned the tooth safely.

'Well . . . kind of . . .' William started.

The Christmasaurus scrunched up his nose and gave a huff.

William looked at his friend and knew he was right. It wasn't accidentally breaking the tooth that had put William's name on the Naughty List, which meant that simply replacing it wasn't the way to put things right. No, William was on the list because he hadn't told his dad the truth. Sometimes it might seem as though lying to your parents is easier than admitting you've done something wrong, but the truth, however hard it is to say, will always set you free.

William felt like his heart sank into his stomach as he took a breath in preparation for what he had to do next.

'Dad, we didn't find the fossil thief because . . .

I AM the fossil thief!'

Bob was silent. He just blinked in confusion. Then he burst out laughing.

'Why are you laughing? I'm serious!' William protested, and Bob could see that he was telling the truth.

'It was an accident. I didn't mean to. I was putting back the fossilized poop, just like you said, when my chair knocked the tooth off the stand and it cracked in half!'

'Cracked in HALF!' Bob gasped.

'I didn't know what to do, so I panicked and put it in my pocket. I've been trying to repair it at home but . . .' William looked at the Christmasaurus, whose blue cheeks flushed a little with embarrassment as he remembered sneezing what was left of the fossil into nothing but dust. 'Well, it's gone.'

'I don't understand, Willypoos. If the tooth from Dino Cove has gone, then what is sitting on that plinth?' Bob asked.

'Well, we flew to Dino Cove tonight to try to get another one . . .'

'And you managed to find one in the middle of the night? That's my boy!' Bob beamed, slightly jealous of the adventure he was imagining they had been on. Then he remembered that William had been lying to him the whole time about being the fossil thief. 'I mean . . . er . . . I'm very disappointed that you didn't tell me the truth, William Trundle,' he said, using William's full name so that William knew he was being serious.

'I know, Dad. I'm sorry,' William said, and he really meant it.

'You can always talk to me, you know. No matter what

you've done or how much trouble you think you might be in, you can always come to me. OK?'

William nodded.

'All right, enough of that – now tell me about this adventure! Was it **dinosawesome**?' Bob chuckled excitedly.

'Not exactly. It was too dark, and the beach was just too big, but then we realized there *was* a dinosaur tooth at Dino Cove – but it was still *inside* a dinosaur's mouth.'

At that, the Christmasaurus opened his mouth with pride, revealing a big gap in his blue gums where his tooth once sat.

Bob turned to look at the new tooth on the plinth.

CLICK!

The door from across the hall suddenly opened and a tall, intimidating figure entered.

'Bob Trundle! What are you doing here?' snapped Mrs Brutelle. She marched towards them, and the Christmasaurus quickly leapt over the security rope, disguising himself among the other dinosaur models and skeletons.

'Your time is up, Trundle. Time to pack your things and –' Mrs Brutelle stopped in her tracks, spotting the gleaming tooth on the plinth.

'**Ta-da!**' Bob said, presenting the tooth.

'I don't believe it!' Mrs Brutelle gasped in astonishment. 'Is that really –'

'A mysterious dinosaur tooth from Dino Cove!' Bob interrupted, giving William a wink as he was, in fact, telling the truth!

Mrs Brutelle's face went as red as a bauble.

'So, Dad gets to keep his job, right?' William said, unable to hide his smile.

'I suppose, seeing as the fossil has been returned . . . Very well, you can stay. For now!' And, with a huff, she marched away to open the museum to visitors.

Bob and William were about to breathe a sigh of relief when her clomping footsteps stopped. Mrs Brutelle whipped round; something had caught her eye.

She peered into the diorama of dinosaurs, gazing past the triceratops, beyond the T-rex, to stare

RIGHT AT
THE CHRISTMASAURUS!

'As you're staying, you can start by removing that awful model at the back there. That blue one. It looks far too unrealistic,' she barked, then stomped off.

The moment the door clicked shut behind her, Bob, William and the 'unrealistic-looking' Christmasaurus fell to the floor laughing. It had been a close call, but one way or another there was a mysterious tooth from Dino Cove back on display at the museum.

❄

'Thanks for your help, Christmasaurus!' Bob said as he gave the dinosaur a goodbye hug in the deserted garden along the side of the dinosaur hall. 'Now, go on – the pair of you deserve a bit of fun after all this drama!'

William and the Christmasaurus didn't need telling twice! They took to the sky, the early morning meaning the streets were still empty of Christmas shoppers. They skimmed along the River Thames, twisted up the Elizabeth Tower towards Big Ben as it **BONGed** eight o'clock, then they soared over the Oxford

Street Christmas lights before arriving back at the Trundles' wonky house.

The Christmasaurus retrieved the Naughty List from the kitchen table and together the best friends watched as William's name faded from the book.

The list was now the lightest it had ever felt as the Christmasaurus tucked it under his elbow. It was Christmas Eve, which meant that his secret mission was over – it was time to head back to the North Pole so that Santa could do his second and final check. All the dinosaur could do now was hope that he'd helped enough Naughty Listers make their way on to the Nice List to restore balance to the scales!

'We did it again, Chrissy! Another Christmas adventure!' William beamed as the Christmasaurus readied himself for the journey home.

The friends hugged goodbye, knowing that in just a few hours the Christmasaurus would be landing back on the house's wonky rooftop along with eight Magnificently Magical Flying Reindeer, a sleigh full of presents and one spectacular man.

But there was no time to waste, so the Christmasaurus

burst into a full sprint and was up and away in two leaps, soaring high over William, who waved until his friend was nothing but a faint speck of blue among the fading stars in the morning sky.

CHAPTER FORTY-ONE

THE GIFT OF SECOND CHANCES

The Christmasaurus burst through the aurora borealis, streaking a trail of dancing colours across the sky above the North Pole like a meteorite pulling a rainbow into the Earth's atmosphere. But, as beautiful as his entrance was, not a single elf, fairy or snowman below saw him, as the whole North Pole was busy making the final preparations for Santa's flight.

The Christmasaurus landed on the edge of Elfville and quietly crept through the deserted streets. With the Naughty List held tightly in his teeth (which didn't ache at all any more!), he headed towards the distant sound of elf-song and the hustle and bustle of the Snow Ranch, where everyone was gathering to witness Santa's famous second check of the lists.

'Gather round, gather round!'

Santa boomed as he came into view outside the grand entrance to his home, looking his very merriest in his extra-thick flying jacket (which kept him warm with its marshmallow lining!).

The watching crowd of Christmassy creatures erupted into applause, and the Christmasaurus used the distraction to zoom up to the window of the reading room and secretly replace the Naughty List on Santa's desk. Then he casually soared back to join the crowd, as though his secret mission to save Christmas had never happened.

'Sprout!' Santa called, and faster than a jingle the tiny elf appeared at his feet.

'Yes, Your Merriness!' Sprout chimed.

'Assemble your team and fetch me the lists and the weighing scales. It's time to check them twice!'

THE CHRISTMASAURUS AND THE NAUGHTY LIST

Santa ordered, and Sprout vanished instantly, only to return a few moments later leading his team of eight elves (Spudcheeks, Snowcrumb, Specklehump, Snozzletrump, Starlump, Sugarsnout, Sparklefoot and himself). They came waddling through the Snow Ranch doors with the two enormous lists and the set of brass weighing scales balanced on their shoulders.

'Do hurry up – it's Christmas Eve, you know! First thing's first, we must weigh the lists. *Elves, place the Nice List!*' Santa ordered like an army general, and his loyal troops obeyed straight away, marching the Nice List towards the scales and placing it on the shiny bowl labelled **NICE**.

The scales tipped immediately as the Nice List sank to the snowy ground with a soft thud, and the crowd cheered.

'Not yet, not yet!' Santa shouted, trying to calm them. 'Elves, place the Naughty List!'

Silence fell.

The tension in the air was as thick as custard as the eight elves heaved the thick book towards the scales and slid it on to the opposite bowl.

The Christmasaurus could hardly bear to watch as the Naughty side of the scales started to fall, lifting the Nice List into the air. Had he failed in his mission? Was all that hard work in helping those children be more thoughtful and considerate wasted? It certainly looked that way as the Naughty List very gently descended towards the snow, and there was a gasp from the crowd.

'Hold it . . . Hold it . . .' Santa muttered, not taking his eyes off the scales – not even to blink!

Suddenly the Naughty List began to rise and the Nice List dropped, until finally both sides of the scales bobbed up and down in the middle before settling in perfect balance.

'Ho, ho, HOORAY!'

Santa cheered and the entire crowd exploded into celebration.

There were cannons blasting baubles over their heads, fairies performing a fly-by (only narrowly avoiding the baubles!), snowmen swapping noses (a snowman tradition), and reindeer parading along the streets.

Over the celebration, the Christmasaurus caught Santa's eye, and Santa gave him a knowing wink.

MISSION ACCOMPLISHED!

The Christmasaurus flew straight into Santa's arms for a huge, squishy hug and let out a roar of pure

happiness, which the thousands of watching elves echoed with a roar of their own (which was, of course, in perfect harmony).

'Well, you certainly took your time!' Santa whispered with a huge smile on his jolly face.

While the elves sang and danced in the streets of Elfville, back inside the Snow Ranch Santa checked the names on his list with his trusty dinosaur at his side.

'I've always known that no child is entirely naughty, nor are they completely nice. Nice children can do naughty things, and naughty children can be nice again, which is why everyone deserves a second chance. And that, my wonderful friend, is the gift you have given them this year. Far more useful than anything I can squeeze down a chimney, that's for certain. Second chances can't be wrapped up and left under a tree, and often they're the hardest thing to give someone, but one second chance can change a life!'

The Christmasaurus thought he might burst with pride.

DONG!

The Gift of Second Chances

A booming bell tolled across the North Pole, drowning out the sounds of the celebration. Everyone instantly fell silent, and a peaceful happiness washed over the crowd as though the bell's chime had some sort of magical power.

'The Christmas Eve Bell! Is it that time already?' Santa gasped at hearing the ancient bell announce that the first child of Christmas Eve had fallen asleep. It was time to fly! He slipped a chocolate Advent calendar out from his inside pocket to double-check the date, then opened the door numbered twenty-four. 'Oh look – it's a little chocolate *me*!' he said chuckling, before eating his own chocolatey face.

'To the sleigh!' he boomed, and at those words the Christmas congregation marched in unison towards the enormous sleigh room, where the most glorious vehicle your imagination could possibly dream of was waiting.

'Presents loaded. Reindeer fed.
Children around the world in bed!'

sang Skysafe, the elf in command of Aerial Operations above the Snow Ranch.

409

'Very good, very good!' Santa smiled, climbing aboard and making himself comfy for the long night ahead. While the Christmasaurus slipped into his harness at the front of the team of reindeer, Santa cleared his throat to say a few words.

> 'My elves, here we are again – another year
>   is over.
> And, while I'd love to chill out in my PJs
>   on the sofa,
> The kids are dreaming patiently and waiting
>   for the sun
> To bring about the morning and, with it,
>   Christmas fun.
> Now we know the Naughty List is just
>   misunderstood,
> And everyone deserves a second chance
>   at being good.
> So let us never let them down,
> For as long as they believe,
> We shall always be here,
> Every year on Christmas Eve.'

At the end of his wonderful words, the elves erupted into applause, and Santa blasted Christmas music from the gramophone in his sleigh, making it magically rise from the floor as though it were somehow floating on the merry notes.

'Ho-ho-GO!'

Santa called, and the Christmasaurus sprang into action, leading the reindeer forward into a gallop. The thumping of hooves and claws thundering across snow and ice made the ground rumble like a powerful engine growling beneath the surface, until they pushed the permafrost away and were striding into the air.

'Merry Christmas!' echoed Santa's resounding voice as he waved to the elves who watched them vanish into the December sky.

❄

And so the Christmasaurus helped Santa deliver presents to everyone on the Nice List, including . . .

A piggy bank for Ronnie Nutbog so he could save **HIS OWN** pocket money.

ONE big book of bedtime stories for Princess Utterly and Princess Truly Snottersworth to **SHARE**.

A brand-new ping-pong paddle for Marvin 'GamerKidd3000' Johnson, along with a cloth to keep their ping-pong trophy nice and shiny.

THE GIFT OF SECOND CHANCES

A new apron for Ella Noying to wear while cooking with her mum.

A karaoke machine for Gemolina Shine, with two microphones so she can sing duets with her new friend, Dorothy Dorkins.

And, for William Trundle, a book called *How to Repair Fossils*, just in case he ever ACCIDENTALLY breaks a priceless, sixty-five-million-year-old artefact again.

The Christmasaurus glowed with pride as he watched Santa disappear down the chimneys of the children he had helped to find their way back on to the Nice List. Thanks to him, they had all rediscovered the importance of being nice and it wasn't only because they wanted presents . . .

OK, maybe it was a little bit because they wanted presents, but mostly it was because, well, it's nice to be nice.

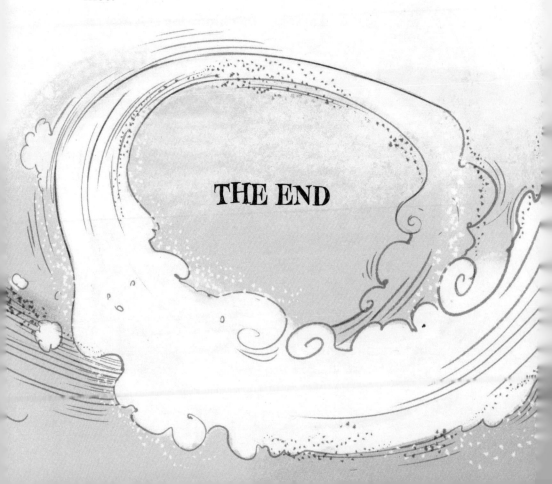

THE END

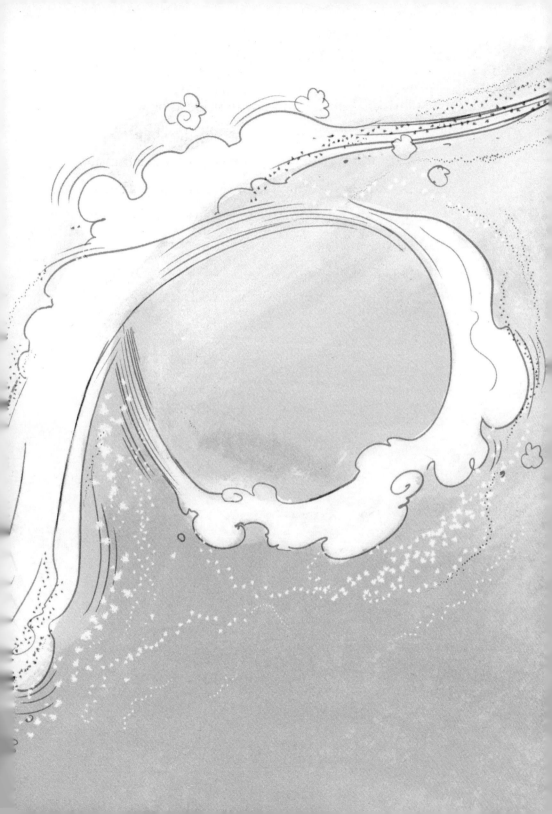

ACKNOWLEDGEMENTS

Creating these books is a huge team effort, of which I play a small part yet get to claim all the glory with my name sprawled across the front in big, shiny, ego-boosting letters for everyone to see! There are so many people who deserve their name to be in large, shiny letters on the cover who will instead have to settle for these small ones in the back pages, but don't be fooled by their size and lack of shininess as the book you have just read (and hopefully enjoyed!) would not exist without . . .

Shane Devries! Thanks for the most magical illustrations. It's an honour to be able to bring stories to life with you.

Jane Griffiths, thanks for leaping into the weird

world inside my head and not running a mile. Thanks to Wendy Shakespeare, Emily Smyth, Mandy Norman, Adam Webling and everyone who works on the editorial, design and production teams, and to Natalie Doherty – the Christmasaurus wouldn't have hatched without you!

Thanks to the following elves at Penguin Random House for all your incredible work and general awesomeness – Sarah Roscoe, Geraldine McBride, Kat Baker, Toni Budden, Rozzie Todd, Sophie Marston, Autumn Evans, Lorraine Levis, Karin Burnik, Becki Wells, Zosia Knopp, Alice Grigg, Maeve Banham, Susanne Evans, Beth Fennell, Lena Petzke, Millie Lovett, Harriet Venn, Sophia Pringle, Lottie Halstead . . . Wow, that's quite a list, but certainly not the naughty one! I'm so incredibly lucky to get to work with you all.

And of course thanks to Tom Weldon, Francesca Dow and Amanda Punter for your continued belief that people might want to read the nonsense that comes out of my brain. I am so grateful.

Stephanie Thwaites, thanks for your constant words of encouragement and enthusiasm for my silly words. You saw potential in them before anyone else!

Acknowledgements

Fletch, the only person who likes Christmas as much as (or potentially even more than) me. The Christmasaurus would never have flown without your belief.

Michael Gracey, working with you provides more inspiration than I could ever dream of.

Rachel Drake, thank you for holding the world together. Aside from how ridiculously hard you work and how much you believe in me, you are also an awesome person!

Thanks to Dave Spearing for the inspiring creative chats.

Thanks to Tommy J. Smith and Nikki Garner for so much festive support and hard work over the years!

Thanks to Danny, Dougie and Harry for supporting/tolerating my literary endeavours.

To Mum and Dad, Carrie and all my family for making my childhood Christmases so magical that I've now written books about it!

Thanks to my increasingly patient and understanding wife, Giovanna, for not only putting up with my Christmas obsession but actually embracing and encouraging it!

And, finally, thanks to our three elves – Buzz, Buddy and Max – for helping me see the world through your wonderful eyes.